Three Furi

M000187654

Cover credit: Southern Exposure Media

For more information contact
Three Furies Press, LLC
30 N Gould St
Sheridan, WY 82801
(509) 768-2249
ISBN ebook: 978-1-950722-84-6
ISBN print: 978-1-950722-85-3
First Edition: September 2021

Gabriela Bianchi

Gabriela Bianchi

Read Me

Gabriela Bianchi

Gabriela Bianchi

Preface

I was nothing, just empty words on paper, until her voice gave me life, excitement, and so much more. She began simply reading my story, adding new words in her soft, lilting voice. But then something happened that neither one of us expected. We fell in love.

But I was wrong.

Gabriela Bianchi

Chapter 1

Awareness seemed to come on unexpectedly. One moment I was nonexistent, and the next my consciousness came into being. I had no explanation for it, nor did I know who was behind it, but I was here nonetheless. *Who was I? What was this place? How did I get here? Why was I here?*

Suddenly, a light appeared before me, interrupting my thoughts as it blinded me with its brightness. I tried to avert my gaze from the searing glow. I could not help but be absorbed by it even though my vision was hazy, making me feel as though I were trying to see through a veil which made the brightness painful to my new eyes.

My mind could not help being coerced to look at it, regardless of the pain it caused me, and as time went on, gazing upon it appeared to become easier as the pain it had caused dulled in its intensity.

The pulsing heat of it was growing into a comfort to me, a companion of sorts. When I tried to rise from my place, to move from my current position, I felt a slight tug. I came to the realization that I could not move at all, but was determined to do so nonetheless. Pulling at my invisible restraints was clearly strenuous as beads of moisture accumulated on me, and created a confusing sensation of simultaneous heat and relief. The realization came to me somehow that all of these sensations felt dull, because I could only register faint reactions to everything around me, but that thought faded to the background as I realized that I had triumphed because my pulling began to take less effort.

My binds felt as if they were slowly coming loose from around me, until I was finally able to break away from them. As I came away from my bonds, I wanted to see where exactly it was that I found myself, and chose to walk slowly at first, to better assimilate the action. Those first steps were shaking and unstable, each one felt more difficult than the last.

After all the effort, there seemed to be nothing to show for it. Nothing but light, no matter where I looked. What I was able to sense seemed dull, as if I was experiencing everything through a cruel veil, which only allowed the whisper of the occurrence. The sun's reflection off the page was the only indicator of the separation between worlds.

I knew about the passage of time, but began to understand it when I could see the shift from day to night. The change in lighting from the outside was my only signal. Wandering along this seemingly blank wasteland, I felt simultaneously weightless, as if I would float away at any moment, and yet also as if I was fixed onto one place in particular, and unable to move at all.

This space was nothing, empty.

Suddenly, the chime of a bell came to me, breaking me out of my thoughts; that in and of itself seemed strange. I was gaining a new awareness. Curiosity overtook me, and so, I decided to listen as the sound of shuffling feet on the floor came to my ears, occasionally followed by a muffled squeak.

Shoes... I thought to myself. These footsteps were light, their squeak being the only evidence of their passing if you were not paying that much attention. But I was. I could hear soft breathing, as well as humming noises, and the almost imperceptible brush of hair against fabric. These piqued my curiosity even more, and I decided to try to take a closer look. Moving as much as I could manage, as well as trying to see if I could walk to the edge, I was proud when I found that I could, but remained within the page.

It was in this way that I was able to see to the outside, and what I saw had stopped me in my tracks.

A girl who appeared to have grown past her teenage years, and was wandering through the forest of her life as a young adult. With red copper hair, eyes so light that they seemed silver, and a constellation of freckles across her face, she looked like what I had imagined the sky to look like. Resplendent. Beautiful. I was absorbed, and felt pin pricks all over that were not at all unpleasant.

Some force unknown to me kept me rooted in place, and I felt compelled to stare after her, to watch as she walked along the shelves, all the while brushing her fingers lovingly along the books' spines, as if they were treasures to be treated delicately. The motion was nearly enough to lull me to sleep, but I fought against it, fought for the opportunity to keep looking at her. As she made her way along the aisle and closer to me, her feet seemed to glide along, I noticed a raised floorboard in her path. Calling out to her seemed useless, because I did not think that she would hear me, and had to watch helplessly as her foot caught on the board's edge to see her stumble and fall to her knees on the floor. I leaned over further, feeling an overwhelming need to go to her, to comfort her when I saw something glisten on her cheek. Tears. I began pushing at the edge of the book, the space that seemed to keep me further away as I tried to get to her as quickly as possible, but all this accomplished was to push the book off the shelf, until I was flying with it, finally tumbling to the floor with a dull thud.

Yes, that was brilliant... I thought as the book lay face down, shrouding me in darkness. I did feel thankful for the carpeting, however, because it prevented what I suspected would be a nasty collision with the visibly hard floor. That was one sharp contrast I did not want to examine.

Not long after, I heard the muffled sound of footsteps approach, and felt a grasp on the edges of the book. The slight external pressure, as well as the internal give, was followed by a pressing sensation as I was lifted into the air. Comforting, and yet dizzying all at once.

My thoughts reeled at all these new sensations. I tried to steady myself, and once that had been accomplished, I was finally able to look into the eyes of the girl. She was even more beautiful up close. There were slight imperfections to her face, like one small scar under her left eye. It didn't mar her appearance in the least, but made her eyes look fuller instead, more alive somehow. This made her all the more lovely to me.

I wonder how she got it....

She looked confused at me—well, at the book—and started flipping through the sheets, tilting her head as she saw what I knew to be blank pages.

"You will not find anything here, girl," I sighed, and the pages around me flicked with my annoyance, making her gasp and drop the book on the floor. In that moment, I knew one thing I

3

certainly hated, being dropped. As I fell, I saw her scared expression, and wondered what had frightened her. Her hands trembled as she picked the book up again.

"Uh, hello?" she called out, her voice uncertain, and I was suddenly dumbstruck by the sweetness of that voice. "I could have sworn I heard..."

Wait. Had she heard me? How? That was not possible. This had never happened before, and even though I knew that I should be terrified, I could not find that emotion within me. My thoughts grappled with the possibility, until I chose to take a risk. "Hello?" I called out, and the word appeared written out on the page, its letters floating all around me until they came to a stop after having found a resting place in the center of the page.

She gasped again, but thankfully, kept a firm grip on the book this time. "Who are you? *Where* are you?" she asked as her hands shook.

Had she heard me? Seen the words written on the page as I did? You scared her, you jerk! I chastised myself. *Fix this.* "Uh, hello? There is no need to fear..."

"Who says I'm scared?" she defended, looking around herself, a look of determination marking her features. "And, you know what? The least you could do is show yourself!"

I laughed. "Alright, so you are not afraid. My apologies. I am right here, by the way."

As she followed the sound of my voice, her eyes finally landed on the book. "Okay... Now I've really gone nuts. I'm talking to a book!"

"I am certain insanity would apply only if the book did not actually talk back."

"Uh yeah, cause having the book talk back to you makes it so much better. *Oh, just shut up Alex!*" she said, clearly chastising herself as she thrust her hand upward. "Okay, so I just won't focus on the fact that I'm talking to a book. Or that the book is talking back to me. How about that? Because that's a completely normal, everyday thing, you know?"

"Look," I interrupted her rambling. "I do not know why I am in here or how this is happening. All I know is that I am here. Stuck. I cannot move beyond these pages, I cannot do anything!"

Something was escalating inside of me, heightening and clouding my mind all at once. The thought of never being able to leave this place made me feel trapped.

"Hey, hey," she soothed, her words muted and slow. "Only one of us is supposed to be freaking out about this situation, and I'm pretty sure that job belongs to me. You can move inside the book though, can't you? It would be cruel if you were twice as stuck."

I began controlling myself then, as I marveled at my intake and output of breath. This was new to me, or had I just never noticed it before? No, that strange sensation in my chest wasn't something I had experienced before. "All I can tell you is that you do not have to be scared, I will not hurt you, and you are not going insane." I supplied, calmer now.

"What's your name?" she asked, and her smile seemed to diffuse my previous agitation.

"I do not have one," I answered simply, and her brow furrowed, making me feel sheepish.

"What do you mean you don't have a name? You have to."

"But I do not," I replied after remembering that I did not have physical indications for my answers.

She pursed her lips then. "Well then, why don't we think of one together?"

Just as I was about to reply, I felt a shudder. And no, it had not been some weak disturbance. This had been strong enough to make my 'stomach' turn. "I... I cannot."

"Hey, why did the book just shake? Are you okay?" she asked, her voice laced with concern.

"Yes, I am fine," I said, shaking off the sickness. "Could you please do it? I do not think I will be of much help, but I would still love to have a name."

She looked thoughtful all of a sudden, with a hint of concern in her eyes. "Well, how about this? I'll mention different names, and you let me know if you like them or not. We'll eliminate the options one by one until we find the right fit for you."

As I listened, I waited for the feeling to return, and I sighed with relief when it did not. "Yes. Thank you."

She smiled in response, and once again I was rendered breathless.

"Okay... Aaron?"

"No. I do not like that name. It does not sound at all like me."

"Glenn?"

"Bah," I grumbled, and she laughed at my tone.

"Leonard?" she offered

"Nah, too nerdy."

She made a face, but kept calling names out, even though none of them sounded right to me. Until finally, one did.

"So, nice to meet you, Wyatt," she said pleasantly, with an encouraging smile on her lips.

"Nice to meet you, too." I smiled in return. I was so happy that I finally had a name, and she had helped me find it.

"Oh, sorry. I'm Alexandra, I prefer Alex though. Okay, then. Look, I... gotta go. This is way too weird."

I was about to ask her not to leave, to figure this out with me, but then decided that her leaving was probably for the best. "Alright. It was nice to finally talk to someone. Thank you."

"Uh... You're welcome," she replied with an indulgent shake of her head. "Hey, I know I found the book open and all, but do you want me to close it for you? I can imagine the sun might be a bit rough at the crack of dawn." Her concern only endeared her more to me.

"Thank you, but no. It does not bother me. I like seeing the sun greet me in the morning and the moon accompany me at night."

She nodded, smiling slightly, and as she closed the door behind her, I noticed an earring on the floor, which I knew must belong to her. She would notice it missing and have to return at some point. The thought made me smile.

Days passed, and there was no sign of her. I resigned myself to the fact that she would never return. That my one day with her would be my last, dismissed as nothing but a dream. I returned to my aimless wanderings.

The door to the shop opened abruptly, casting a shadow that called my attention, and I looked up to see the girl I had come to think of as a dream.

"Thanks for coming with me, Jess. I just need some time to regroup, you know? Anyway, this is the last place where I remember having my earring." Alexandra's voice rang in my ears and my breath caught.

I could not help but notice that something was wrong, so I decided to keep listening as they shuffled along. A second voice giggled conspiratorially, adrenaline making the sound barely audible. Two beings became visible from my vantage point as their shadows played with the sunlight, and both seemed to be searching for the missing piece of jewelry along the aisles.

"Are you sure you'll be alright? Where are we anyway? You know what, never mind. Where we should really be going is to the hospital and then to the police. He can't keep doing this to you!"

"Hey, can we just focus on the topic at hand here, please? My home issues aren't going anywhere anytime soon." Alexandra sighed dejected, and the friend, Jessica, exhaled forcibly.

"Fine. But if you don't call the cops soon, don't be surprised when you find them at your door one day anyway. Uh... what is this place?"

I could tell that this Jessica was the type of person that could never focus on one subject alone.

"I think it's some abandoned bookstore or something," Alexandra explained as she walked toward me, picked up the book and peaked inside. "And we are here because.... Because I want to show you something," Alexandra responded excitedly as she walked toward me. She picked up my book, held it tightly in her arms, and then peaked inside. "Hey, Wyatt?" she whispered. "How are you today?"

"I am well, Alexandra. How are you?" I asked, warily.

"I'm well, thanks. Hey, do you think you might want to meet my friend?"

"Why?" I wondered, carefully.

She looked at me then, well, at the pages, and her expression changed from excited to sheepish. "Nothing, never mind," she replied, and then turned toward her friend, shaking her head. "You

7

know what, Jess, why don't we forget this and go to the movies instead?"

"What, don't tell me you're freaking out over this? You're the one that wanted to come here!"

"I'm not! I just thought about it, and there are better options to spend my hideout day than to be stuck in an abandoned book-store."

Jess huffed and seemed to relent. "Okay, but *only* because we need to get you out of your funk. Unless you want to go to the police.... We still have time, you know?"

"No. Let's just get out of here. Please?"

"Alright, alright, we'll leave. What is it with you..." her friend's voice trailed as she looked around. They then walked to the door,

Alexandra cast a glance my way, which let me know that they were leaving, as well as communicated an apology.

I thought of her, of how much I wanted to be a comfort for her, as well as the worthlessness of my concern when I couldn't do anything to help her... I wondered what could be bothering her. From what I'd heard her friend say, it was likely some problem at her home, but what? And with whom? I felt a sudden rush of anger toward this unknown peril; as well as an overwhelming need to protect her from anything that might cause her harm. But how could I when I was stuck between these pages, when she wouldn't even open up to her own friend. I could only dare to hope, how-ever futilely, that she'd confide in me.

A few hours later, I heard the door open softly, and her all too familiar footsteps approaching me. "Hello Alexandra," I greeted, pleasantly.

"Hey Wyatt... Look, I'm sorry for before, it's just that she was asking where I was the other day, and she wouldn't accept what I'd told her so—"

"Do not worry," I placated. "It was just unexpected."

She looked sheepish as she shuffled her feet. "My bad. I am an idiot. Forgive me?"

"So, are you okay with this now?" I asked, with an audible smirk.

"This... what?" she asked, a confused expression on her face.

"Me, the fact that I'm in here, and that you and I can some-how communicate?"

She put her hand to her neck and pursed her lips. "Huh, well... Not really, but I keep coming here, and you apparently keep talking to me, so... I'm just gonna wing it and see what happens."

I laughed. "Well, good. Can I ask you something?"

"If it's about a certain subject, I don't want to talk about it. It's fine. Really," she rushed.

"I really hope you'll trust me one day," I told her, and she looked at the book with glossy eyes as she played with the page edges.

This was as close as I would ever get to touching her. My happiness was short-lived as I caught sight of her demeanor, her eyes had sunk in, and her face looked haggard and sallow. She was clearly exhausted.

"You should try to rest," I suggested.

"Yeah, I think I should. I haven't been getting much sleep lately. I'll just rest my head on the desk for a while." She sat down at a desk nearby and rested her head on one of her arms, the other extended as if trying to reach for me.

I smiled as I saw sleep take over her and felt suddenly drowsy myself, so I decided to rest as well. "Sweet dreams, Alexandra."

"Sweet dreams, Wyatt," she mumbled.

I dozed off soon after, lulled into my first fitful sleep by her. Soon after, there was no sound other than our breathing.

The following morning, I arose to the bright light of day-break as it peeked through the pages, like my own makeshift sun-rise, and saw Alexandra lying fast asleep. The sun seemed to re-flect off of her hair and skin, making her glow. It took my breath away. A soft exhale escaped her lips, followed by a slight whim-per. I felt her tighten her grip on the book almost painfully.

"Alexandra... Wake up. You are having a nightmare," I whis-pered, not wanting to frighten her further.

She stirred awake with a gasp, her breath nothing but sharp inhales and exhales. Her eyes turned crystalline, seemingly transparent, and within that transparency, I saw a pain so acute, that I could feel it myself.

"Are you alright?"

"Ugh, I hate that question," she sighed, looking upward, trying to rid herself of her tears. "I'm fine. It was just a nightmare. Thanks for waking me up."

"You are welcome," I told her, assessing that she truly was alright. Her breathing was slowing, and her complexion seemed to be regaining color, so I decided to let it go.

As she blinked away the sleep and tears from her eyes, she turned her head toward a large window, and jumped. "I have to get out of here!" she exclaimed.

"Why? What is happening?" I asked, my anxiety escalating with her movements. I didn't want her to leave.

"People, genius! In case you didn't know, I'm not exactly supposed to be in here," she explained as she stood and started looking for an exit.

"There is a door at the back that you could use," I suggested.

"Thanks," she sighed, darting for the door with nervous energy.

"Wait!" I yelled after her, making her stop cold.

"What? Do you hear someone coming? Oh man, I am in so much trouble!"

I instantly felt guilty for scaring her yet again, which made my tone shameful. "I am sorry. No one is coming. I was just going to ask if I would see you again. Also, no one apart from you and your friend have ever come here. No one ever has really. You need not worry."

She looked at me incredulously and then sighed. "You could have mentioned that before, you know? I'd have freaked out a bit less, don't you think? I'll come back soon, though I'm clearly out of my mind."

"I will let you know that I am smiling."

"Aww, that's sweet... I think. Okay, I really should leave now. See you later, Wyatt," she said, waving.

I began to wave back, smiling as I managed to lift the page fully, and not just a slight flick. "Until we meet again, Alexandra," I relented.

She smirked as she left, the door closing with a dull click behind her.

I splayed, literally drifting on air, as images of her played in my mind. The stubborn set of her lips, her piercing silver eyes, which spoke of quiet strength. I wanted nothing more than to get to know her, and for her to get to know me.

Who am I kidding? I do not even know who I am... But I could build myself up; make myself into a good person, worthy of friendship... Maybe even worthy of love?

Chapter 2

Who was I fooling? I was a figment. Just written words. I had no business even contemplating a life with her. I did not expect the girl to "visit" again, because I thought this would prove to be too much for her, and that she would think it best to forget about all of it. About me. I could not be selfish however, I had to stop thinking about my problems, and begin to think about helping Alexandra.

What had made her so nervous, so distant? It was true that she possessed a reserved air, but at some points she seemed out-right scared, as if expecting to pay a price for simply speaking.

I wanted to help her conquer those fears, as well as the thoughts that surely poisoned her mind and spirit. Hopefully, she would be willing to accept what little help I could give her, but all I had to do was think of those innocent looking silver eyes, that smile, and I could not keep from trying my hardest to chip away at least a little bit of the pain that kept the real Alexandra buried underneath. That made my goal clear. To stop wallowing in my misfortune, and focus my energy and endless time on her, which I would do gladly for the sake of one true smile.

But all I had to do was hear that click and shuffle, and my mood lifted, somehow knowing it was her without having to see her silhouette. *Whoever thought that a door opening would become the highlight of my day?*

She walked straight over to the book, and tapped her finger on the spine as a form of knock. It was not necessary, but very much appreciated. "Yes, Alexandra?"

"When are you going to stop calling me Alexandra? It's Alex. Just Alex, okay? Short, sweet, and to the point. All my friends call me that," she explained, lifting a lone corner of her lips, which made me smirk.

"Might I be correct in thinking that you want us to be friends?"

"Of course, and stop talking so properly," she mocked, furrowing her brow. "This is the 21st century, and I am *not* in English class."

I laughed. "I apologize, but this is how I speak. I have tried changing it, but have not had much practice."

"Fine. But we're going to work on it, got it?"

"Yes. Now, might I ask what brings you here today?"

"You're not happy to see me?" she asked, dejectedly.

"My dear Alexandra, I am very happy that you have chosen to visit today. I only ask because it seems that you are spending nearly a lot of time here this week. What about your family?"

She turned solemn at that, so quiet you could hear the breeze from the cracks underneath the door.

"Please forgive me, Alexandra. I meant no offense..."

"You didn't offend me, Wyatt. It's just that... Well, I don't like thinking about my parents." She shrugged, her voice hollow.

"I won't push. You tell me only if and when you are ready."

"Thank you," she said, hanging her head. She began to say something but immediately stopped, her lips seeming to stitch together in a show of silence.

"Is something wrong? You can tell me, Alexandra. You are safe here," I vowed, replacing my original thought. I had wanted to tell her that she was safe with me, but I thought that this might do more harm than good. She mumbled uncertainly in response, her voice unstable. "Shh... Remember that you are safe, Alexandra. Nothing can harm you here."

"Can I stay here? You know, permanently?" she asked suddenly, her question taking me by surprise.

"But what of your family? I am certain they would worry," I commented, despite the fact that I wanted to agree immediately to her request.

"I don't have a family. Only people that watch over me because the state says it's their job, and they get a check every month. I think they'd lie and say that I was still living with them, even if I disappeared. Other than that, I'm alone. All I have is Jess and.... You," she answered, anger and sadness simmering in her voice, her cheeks turning a slight pink. "I'm sorry, I shouldn't have asked. It's not your problem. It's mine. It's not like you can help me right?"

As she waved her hand dismissively, I came to realize that her brushing me off. That angered me, but I figured it was her nerves talking so I paid no mind to it. "Are you afraid?" I hedged.

She nodded, her eyes slowly filling with tears again, even as she tried to fight them.

"Alexandra, you have nothing to be afraid of. You can stay here for as long as you would like. I just imagined that you would want to go home, that is all. The only reason I never asked you to stay was because I never expected you to want to. I knew that you had a family that you needed to return to, and that I had no right to ask you to stay."

"But I don't," she said angrily, and that only angered me further.

The thought of her being on her own, having to act in accordance to the whim of careless people day to day made me wish more than ever that my confinement was non-existent. I decided that I could not let her go back there, that I wanted her to stay with me for as long as she wanted. "Stay here, with me. You do not have to return. I promise." As soon as the words left me, I saw the tears she had tried so hard to hold back.

She immediately began to wipe her eyes. "I'm sorry for crying. I'm such a wimp," she deflected, laughing shortly. "So, where would I sleep? Any suggestions?"

I shook my head for my lone benefit. "It is your choice, but I have never seen anything that even resembles a bed in here."

"I'm sure I can find something," she said, and went on her hunt.

I did the only thing I could do. Wait.

"I found it!" she shouted happily from one of the rooms, after a long while. What she dragged back with her was not a bed by any standards, but a flat, uncomfortable looking piece of foam, and I immediately wanted to protest. "Are you sure you will be able to rest on that? It looks unbelievably uncomfortable."

"Of course. Besides, I found some cushions in a closet nearby, I just couldn't drag this over and carry them all at once, you know?"

"I imagine not," I smirked.

"So, I think I'm pretty much set," she sighed, after placing the mattress near the old furnace. It was a great open space, one that ensured her comfort.

"You did good work, Alexandra," I said, impressed as I glanced at her arrangement. "But should you not build a fire if you are going to sleep in front of the fireplace?"

"I was getting to that!" she defended, clicking her tongue.

I laughed. "Whatever you say, girl."

She took the book in her arms and stuck her tongue out at me. "Has anyone ever told you that you're a bit of a smart-ass?"

"You just did, didn't you?" I laughed. "Other than that, no one has had the pleasure of listening to my wit."

"Lucky me..." she mumbled, halfheartedly.

"Yes, lucky you, and lucky me for having you around," I said, sincerely.

"Oh, see? Now you're just kissing up."

"Kissing up?" I asked, confused.

"Brown nosing? Saying things to get on my good side," she explained.

"Me, never!" I gasped, laughing. "But in all seriousness, Alexandra. You are the first person I have had any contact with, and I cannot tell you how grateful I am for that."

She blinked, surprised. "Oh, well, you're welcome. It's really no problem. You're a great person."

"As are you," I pointed out, and had the pleasure of seeing her blush again, scarlet blanketing her freckles like a veil.

She laughed awkwardly, placing her hand on her neck in a shy gesture. "Well, it's getting late," she said, gesturing to the darkening sky outside the window. "What do you say we wrap this up and sleep? We'll talk again tomorrow."

I could have spoken to her all night, but I could see that she was having trouble keeping her eyes open, and her demeanor changed from energetic to languid. "Of course. You rest, Alexandra. Goodnight."

"Goodnight, Wyatt. Sweet dreams," she yawned.

I spent my time counting her breaths until she was finally asleep, keeping watch over her dreams in case she needed me to rescue her from not so favorable ones. As I drifted off, I vowed right then that I would always be there for her.

As the glow of morning sunlight touched the edges of my pages, I could also feel Alexandra's arms around the book. *She must have fallen asleep with it*, I thought. I lost myself while staring at her; all the while taking in the details of her face.

"You are her constant..." a voice whispered out of nowhere, breaking me out of my reverie.

"Who said that? Who are you?" I asked, alarmed. Searching for the source of the voice, I found no one.

"Someone you'll know soon enough. But first, you must help her."

"How?" My voice betrayed my anxiety. I wanted nothing more than to help the girl.

"Be whatever she needs you to be. If you do this, she will open up. If you do this, you will be free. Ask her to write your story."

"Can she do that? And how would I get her to do it?" I would love it if Alexandra wrote for me. If she wrote the path that I would take, if she became my way to freedom and all of its virtues.

"First," the voice interjected, "you must help get her on the path to believe in herself. The rest will follow. Maybe even..." She laughed. "Yes, maybe even love. But neither of your roads will be easy. There are many obstacles, as well as foreseeable danger ahead for both of you."

Her words caused an uncomfortable twisting that I felt in the very core of me. "What danger?"

"I am sorry, but there are too many paths to tell which is which. All I can say is that your decisions will dictate what will lie ahead for you."

I exhaled in frustration. "Alright. So I'll just concern myself with the present. For now."

"You should go to her. She needs you," the voice told me, and immediately my attention was on Alexandra. Her restlessness, the fear etched on her face...

"Alexandra..." I called, trying to awaken her as gently as possible so as not to frighten her. A soft moan sounded from her lips, her breathing quickened and led to small sobs. My heart broke for her. What could possibly be wrong? What could have made her react this way? The first thing that came to mind was to make the book warm, imagining everything I felt radiate outward, heating everything around me comfortably, while trying to make my emotions known to her as physically clear as I could, and she stiffened, awakening soon after.

"Mm... What happened?" she asked, her voice quiet.

"I think you might have been having a bad dream."

"Another one..." she trailed off, ending in a frustrated grunt. "They're just dreams I have, pretty bad ones, but just dreams."

"You can talk to me. You know that, right? It might help you."

She closed her eyes and took in a breath. "Thank you, but I don't think I can talk about it right now. You know, even though it's crazy, I feel safe here."

That little sentence made me so happy. "I am glad, Alexandra. And you can talk whenever you are ready to."

She took a big breath, and I heard relief and trust within it. "I guess I can tell you a little bit... You won't go blab about it to anyone about it, will you?"

"Only to these blank pages," I teased in a blasé tone, hoping to lift her mood, if only a little.

"Well, are they trustworthy?" she followed, smiling.

"Most of the time... But do not worry, I will demand the strictest secrecy from them. So, what would you like to do today?" I asked after a pause.

"Huh, I think this place could use a bit of life, don't you?"

"There is a talking book, and now one human. How much more 'life' could you want?" I mocked. But really, the idea of sharing my world, my Alexandra, with anyone else filled me with dread.

"Aww, you don't like to share..." she mocked me in return. "You know, any other person would go running for the hills at your weirdly possessive word choices... I must be insane."

"I apologize. I did not mean to sound possessive, but you are the first person to talk to me, and I am not ready to let that go just yet."

"You don't have to, Wyatt. I'm not going anywhere. I've already accepted this madness, remember?" she chuckled softly.

"I seem to remember something similar to that happening, yes." I laughed.

"So, yeah. Do you have any neighbors? Any other people in these books you talk to? Any girls in need of adventure?" Alexandra asked, conversationally.

I loved how playful she was, but the idea of someone else contacting her made me feel wrong for some reason. As wrong as it was, sharing her just didn't feel right to me. "None, at all. At least, no one has spoken out, so I am fairly certain that I am the only oddity here."

"Nope, definitely not the weirdest book here." She laughed as she placed me on a desk, and walked over to my neighboring shelves, to look at various titles. "This one is an old-timey anatomy book, and those can get pretty weird," she said, making a face at me, to which I burst into laughter.

"I will trust you on that."

"Really, look," she stated, demonstrating the cover of 'Living Intestines, And The Body That Loves Them' with a sarcastic expression on her face.

"I thought informative books were supposed to have serious titles. This one's just weird..." I laughed again.

"You have a nice laugh, you know that? It's very calming," she said in a hushed tone.

"Thank you, Alexan..." I began, and was brought up short by her glare. "Alex."

"That's better," she nodded approvingly, and her face suddenly contorted with pain, tears flooding her eyes. I could see the strain from her trying to fight them off. "Alexandra, what is wrong?" I panicked.

With a shaking hand, she slipped off the shoulder of her shirt, revealing a grave looking bruise that marred her beautiful skin. "Don't worry about it."

I took a deep breath to calm myself, but in reality, I was seething. "Please tell me what happened," I nearly begged. "Why are there bruises on you? Who hurt you?"

She blew out a breath and her eyes watered even more. "My dad... He..."

I stopped her. "Your father did this to you? Why?" I exclaimed, my frustration threatening to bubble over. Now more than ever, I felt an overwhelming need to protect her. "What can I do, Alex? Tell me, please. I want to help you."

She looked at me, her eyes tired and inflamed from crying. "I don't think there's anything you could do for me, Wyatt. I have to deal with my own problems."

"To hell with that!" I exclaimed, to which her eyes widened. "I'm sorry, but please don't expect me to sit by while this is happening and act like it doesn't bother me. That offends me, Alexandra. I... I care about you."

She looked stunned, her cheeks coloring with shock and incredulity. "You know what I wish?" she asked calmly after a long silence, undoubtedly trying to dissipate the feeling that hung around us.

"What?" I asked soothingly, trying to quiet the restlessness that seemed to hang over us.

"I wish that I never had to go back. That I never had to set foot in that house again," she said longingly.

"You won't have to," I said fervently.

To which she blinked, her eyes showing confusion. "What do you mean?"

I steeled myself. "Well, I already told you that you could stay here. You know that. Now I'll just add that you can stay here for as long as you need to."

"Yeah, I do. Thank you. I just hoped that..."

"I know," I soothed, knowing that she wanted there to be the possibility of a home filled with love and understanding. What any home should have, at least according to things I had heard. I vowed that we would build it together. If she would have me.

Her eyes became rivers bound to overflow.

"Hey," I called, wishing that I could touch a hand to her cheek and could feel the softness of her skin without pages. "No tears, alright?"

She looked up at the ceiling and sniffled, trying to stifle them. "Okay. I'm done. I'm done."

"What do you say to something to help you forget, my dove?"

"Your dove?" she asked, confused.

Embarrassment struck me instantly as the name had come to me so suddenly, that I did not censor myself. "I apologize. Forget the name..."

"No. I like it. Thank you," she said, a smile rising to her lips like a sunrise.

"You are most welcome... my dove," I dared, wanting her to get accustomed to my endearments, as she would receive many, because I wanted her to know that she was deserving of them. And of so much more.

Chapter 3

We spent the following day laughing, talking, and just enjoying each other's company. It was wonderful to get the opportunity to see her laughing, happy, and carefree; moods that suited her beautifully. As we chatted, she turned bright eyes toward me, charged with thrill.

"I'll be right back."

I gazed after her, and laughed at the determined look to her as she began to search within dusty bookshelves.

She downright ransacked them in her excitement. "Oh, come on... This was a bookstore. You'd think there'd be... Aha!" she exclaimed triumphantly, holding a couple of pencils in hand.

Coming to sit on her knees beside my book, she poised her pen upon the page, and the memory of the voice drifted back to me... *Ask her to write your story...*

"Alexandra—"

"Wyatt, can I—" she said timidly, pencil held aloft, and we both laughed at having spoken over each other.

"You go first," I conceded.

"Well," she pondered audibly. "I was wondering if maybe I could help you by... Writing for you?" Her words made me smile instantly, because I wanted this more than I could have ever imagined. Not knowing of my earnest desire to have her write for me, she began to ramble. "I mean, I could just write simple things. It's not like I'd be that good at it. But I just—"

"Alexandra, please stop. I would love it if you wrote for me."

She smiled in response. "It would be a pleasure." She blushed, smiling as she focused on the pages in front of her, her brow furrowing, her tongue poking out a bit in concentration.

I laughed as I watched her, at which she just stuck her tongue out at me.

"First things first. What would you like to look like? Blond? Brunette? Redhead? Shaggy? Clean cut?" she asked, her voice firm and determined.

I thought of this for a minute, wanting to look decent and presentable. Yet, as I recounted the description I thought would most suit me, I noticed Alexandra flinching. "What is wrong?" I asked, concerned by her reaction.

She shook her head, her eyes seemingly returning from some horrible scene that played in her mind. "N-nothing. Don't worry about it."

"I will not forget about this, but I will not mention anything about it if it bothers you. For now. You will have to speak to me at some point however, Alexandra."

"I know, I know," she sighed, taking the book in hand and sitting on what was now her chair, her face adopting a steely expression. Her eyes betrayed her nerves, however, but managed to look determined nonetheless.

"There she is. My brave girl. I knew she was in there," I said with a smile in my voice, but my next words treaded carefully. "You can talk to me."

"Where would I start?" she asked, bowing her head as she took deep breaths to calm herself.

"Start with whatever would be easiest to share. Don't worry. I'm here for you," I said, trying to calm her further.

"Well... Things weren't always like this. I think I should start off by saying that."

Her nervousness became obvious as she rubbed absently at her arms, and my heart ached for her as I thought of her admission, but I could not dwell on it, because I knew that would not help her. I needed to help get her to a place where she would talk about her problems freely and openly. It was my hope that someday she might even be able to heal from them.

"After mom left, it was like dad turned into a zombie. He'd zone out from time to time, and on the days he would come back to reality, he would shout at me that I was never good enough. That I was the reason why mom had left."

The sadness in her voice seemed to permeate everything around us, until it finally made its way into me. "Why would he do that?" I seethed as anger took hold of me, and at that moment, I yearned for physical hands, as well as something to strike. I hated the idea of Alexandra being in that situation, and wanted nothing more than to avenge her.

"I don't know," she shrugged. "I guess I learned pretty early on not to pay attention to it, but all that got me was the beginning of him forcing me to pay attention. He'd grip me, shake me, anything to get me to look him in the eye, when all I wanted to do was to leave."

"Did you?" *Well, wasn't that a stupid question...*

"I did try. Really. I'd packed a bag and snuck out one night, but one of his asshole bar buddies saw me and ratted me out. Dad dragged me home after that, and I've been stuck there ever since, because he doesn't want to lose his income. Though he could just lie and say that I was still under his roof anyway, so what's the point? The few days that I've been here with you have been a nice vacation from all of that, but I'm scared that he'll find me at some point." Her voice shook, and she was tapping her foot absentmindedly. It appeared that her nerves were gaining hold on her tightly, refusing to let go. Her reactions mirrored those I had read of in some of the literature pertaining to medicine, but because of my focus on her, most of that information had slipped my mind.

"I will not let him get to you, do you hear me?" I asserted fervently. "We will find a way, but the first issue at hand here is that I cannot, in good conscience, allow you to go back there. Not after what you have just told me. I would sincerely prefer that you consider staying here."

"But what if he finds me?" she asked, her voice cracking in a nervous high pitch.

"Then we shall have to leave. Together. I will not abandon you, Alexandra. There is no chance that I would ever leave you to deal with this."

Her eyes began to swim with emotion at my declaration, and she turned her head in embarrassment. "Thank you."

"There is no need to hide from me, much less run from me. We are friends, after all. Are we not?" Those words turned a bitter flavor, because I wanted to be more than just a friend to her, but she smiled slowly and wiped off her tears.

"Yes, thank you. Now let's get to writing you a life."

I laughed. "Go on ahead."

Alexandra began by writing my surroundings first, giving me forests, rivers, as well as a house to live in. She then asked if I would like any neighbors, but I was not ready for other people just yet. In reality however, I didn't want to become distracted from her. The action of her writing was peaceful, creating what felt like a bubble that we lost ourselves in, where nothing could disturb us.

"You're sure you don't want anyone to keep you company? I could make you friends. A guy friend you could talk to? A... girl?"

I heard a slight catch in her throat at the end of that question. It got my hopes up that maybe she could become as invested in me as I had become in her; in whatever this was, really. "No, all I need is you," I offered, sincerely, and her face caught the color I had come to love to see, a pink sunrise on her cheeks.

"Alright, then," she deflected, and began writing.

She had only written a few sentences, but as I looked around myself, I no longer saw a blank space, but a beautiful scene around me. My home. And it was all thanks to her. There was a house, sturdy and lovely, surrounded by trees. And in the distance, I could see some splashing. A river? Not long after, the view around me became stunning as she kept adding bits and pieces, all the while asking me what I would like, and making it appear.

Her eyes widened as she saw things emerge as she wrote them, the pages coming to life in front of her eyes with vivid imagery and color as the words appeared on the page. "Whoa..."

"I second that," I whispered in wonder, as I saw everything she had created. It was perfect.

"Now we just have to work on you," she said cheerfully as she set pencil to paper, and I felt myself knit together as she wrote the words, making me appear.

All the while, I felt the caress of her hushed words as she mumbled to herself. I looked on, and I saw myself come together, two arms, two legs, one torso and so on. I was also amazed to hear my heart beat for the first time, strong and steady in my ears. "Wow," I breathed, touching my chest, which made her smile.

"What?"

"My... heart. I can feel it. I can hear it beating in my ears. It is incredible."

"Well, I'm happy for you, Wyatt. Should I keep going?" she asked, smiling proudly.

"Yes, please..." I agreed, marveling at all of these new sensations.

She added to my personality traits next, making me brave, expressive, and caring. She even mixed in some quirks, which made me laugh. She made me loyal, loving, dependable, she also made me strong willed, and sensitive. Somehow, I knew that these were traits which she yearned to find, and the fact that she had given them to me made me feel closer to her; a bond was clearly forming between creator and creation. I felt as if I could not live without her.

Suddenly she gasped, her hand flying to her chest and her eyes going wide as she gripped her blouse.

"Wh- What was that? It felt like a jolt," she wondered, agitated as she felt what I could only think of as a correlating shock in mine.

"I think it is a bond of some sort. Do you not feel it?" I replied, and her eyes widened further, recognition making them glow.

"Yes. I mean, I think so. But what does it mean?"

"I do not know, but I feel as though whatever does happen, one will not go through anything without the other knowing. I also feel like I need to be near you. Do you not?"

A nervous nod was her only answer.

"I have to look after you, Alexandra. You will not be alone ever again."

Her eyes began to tear. "Is this really happening? I'm really dreaming this, aren't I?"

I laughed, rustling my pages to caress her cheek, and I relished in the fact that I could.

"Wow, when did you learn to do that?" she asked, her glistening eyes wide with shock.

"You can do anything you set your mind to."

"Well, that's true enough," she said, blushing all the while. "Okay, now that you have a body, let's get to work on your face. Sound good?"

I nodded and smiled, happy that she could actually see me now.

As she set to work, sculpting eyes, a nose, ears, cheekbones and lips, I felt each of those materializing on me, and reached to touch them. In my excitement, I ran to one of the mirrors inside my new home, and looked at my reflection.

There I was... The muscled build, the sharp angles to my face, black hair, green eyes and caramel toned skin.

This was Wyatt. This was... me.

Chapter 4

The following day, I awoke not really knowing if I had slept, a faint excitement making time pick up speed, while also making it so that I could not focus on anything as I headed directly toward a mirror in *my home*, to see my reflection. I still could not believe that all of this had been gifted to me. The image which reflected back to me appeared blurred, but was very much present, one which bespoke of my endless gratitude to Alexandra.

"Uh oh, I think you might be becoming one of those guys that can't step away from a mirror for more than five seconds. I might have created a monster." She laughed as she appeared, seemingly from nowhere, rubbing sleep from her eyes as she peered into my new home.

"I apologize, but can you fault me?" I defended as I looked on in wonder, but sobered as an inkling of concern settled in my mind. "I fear I might lose all of this..."

"I'm just kidding," she cut in, "but I really believe this will stick. I can't imagine what this must be like for you though, see-ing—having a reflection for the first time. What do you see?"

"I see... myself, but as if I were faded? It makes me feel as though this could all disappear at any moment, but even if it did, I would be ever thankful for them." I smiled, and was happy to know that she would finally see it. "It is also very strange, being able to sense through touch. Almost overwhelming. And I feel that I must apologize to you." The rapt look in her eyes, clouded over with confusion, and I felt the need to elaborate. "You have given me so much, and I have yet to give you anything in return."

"You have already done so much for me, Wyatt. Your pres-ence is more than enough for me," she said sincerely, but I could see the sadness behind it, and I wanted nothing more in that mo-ment but to avenge her. To make the lowlife who had harmed her feel her pain multiplied, but I could not focus on that at the moment, because she needed me. "Well, maybe I could help you. I mean, if you like," she finished.

"Yes, of course. I would appreciate your help greatly."

"Okay. Hm... I think that sensory integration therapy would be the most sensible route, but since I am nowhere near that kind of know-how, we'll have to play it by ear. Do you trust me?"

"Without a doubt," I said quickly.

She blew out a breath and furrowed her brow in concentration, and soon her words became one with the page. At this point our next task became exercise for me, to help me assimilate everything I was given. Sight, smell, touch, and hearing were all targeted. I was immersed in overwhelming sounds that would weaken and strengthen at intervals, my hearing adjusting with every change. I then began to feel bearable shocks running from my head to my toes, livening up each extremity they coursed through. These shocks also seemed to have sparked my sense of smell, because I became suddenly aware of the musty paper and dust smell of my surroundings as they tickled my nose and made me sneeze. We both laughed at that, and the sound seemed sharper and more defined now.

"This... I never thought that I could have this! Thank you!"

She smiled shyly. "You're a fast learner, but we might need to have various sessions to get you to where you need to be. And you're welcome."

I felt instantly mortified. "Forgive me, Alexandra. You have given me so much, and I have yet to give you anything in return. I cannot thank you enough."

"You don't need to thank me, Wyatt, and you don't owe me anything either. You being here to talk to is enough for me," she said sincerely as she smiled at me, but I saw the sadness hidden behind it.

I wanted nothing more than to avenge her. To make the low-life that had harmed her feel her pain tenfold. But I couldn't focus on that now, because she needed me. "Are you alright? I know you hate to be asked, but..."

"I know. You can't help yourself." She smirked. "I'm fine though, I just have a lot on my mind, and I know what you're going to say. I think I will share at some point, okay?"

"I will wait however long you need," I replied honestly.

"You know, it's too bad you're stuck in there," she whispered, blushing, and I was beginning to see this as a regular occurrence with her.

"It's fine. What would I do out there anyway, right?" I mused aloud.

"Hey, I'm sure you'd manage yourself just fine."

"Maybe," I acquiesced, and all of a sudden, I started to feel a rumble in my stomach.

"Whoa, I heard that. I think someone's hungry. Sorry, I wasn't thinking," she said, and promptly set to work writing my first meal. "How does chicken soup with cheddar crackers sound? Maybe some water? I don't want to risk hurting your stomach with anything too heavy too soon, you know?"

"Uh, alright. This feels so strange..." I commented, distracted.

"I know, I'll help you now," she said, and as she proceeded to work a steaming bowl appeared in front of me with the crackers next to it.

No sooner did I have them in front of me then I began to devour the items ravenously, and it seemed as if I began to adjust to this indulgent necessity rather quickly as my mind registered the temperature and told me to pace myself to avoid burning my mouth. My body did not care nonetheless, because I needed this. The flavors seemed to build a symphony that worked together in harmony.

"Easy there, fella, you have to pace yourself or you'll regret it later," she warned with a giggle, at which point I stopped when I felt a slight discomfort in my belly that only seemed to escalate.

"You had to mention it," I whined, gripping my stomach.

"That's a basic reaction to eating like you just did. Welcome to the world of bodies, my friend," she said knowingly, her hands raised as if in surrender.

"Thanks..." I replied sarcastically.

"Sorry! You'd better get used to it though," she exclaimed.

"So, what do I do now?" I groaned.

"Just wait it out, I'm afraid. The best way is to distract yourself from it. Hey, I could write you a friend, would that help?"

The thought intrigued me, but the thought of sharing Alexandra felt wrong, worse than I thought it would. "That is not necessary, but thank you."

"Why not? You might want someone else to talk to. You'll be getting bored in no time with just me here."

"Never," I vowed. "When will you learn to see what a wonderful person you are? The person I am certain that everyone would see if you chose to open up to them." Shock overtook me as the words that had come out of me registered in my mind. Knowing that she had every right to live her life outside of the one she lived here, a life away from me, did not endear me to the possibility. I knew that it was wrong, but I could not help myself. I wanted her with me always, but I also knew that I would have to let her go, regardless of whether or not she ever chose to leave. "Alexandra. When will you see what a wonderful person you are? I can see it, despite the fact that we haven't known each other for long." My arms ached to hold her.

"I don't know, but I do know that you're right. I cannot allow my circumstances to dictate my life. I promise to try. I mean, I already took the first step by leaving, right?"

"Absolutely," I agreed fervently.

"Okay, no more pity parties from now on. I promise." She sighed and gave the beginnings of a smile. "So, how are you liking your house so far? Did I do well?"

"You did wonderfully! I love it, thank you!" I exclaimed, happiness radiating from within.

"You're welcome." She smiled my favorite smile, the one that seemed to make her shine from within, and it made me think that she could truly be happy here.

Could it be because of me? Or could it simply be relief at being away from those that caused her pain? I knew that I was being presumptuous at even posing such a possibility, reading too much into it. I was in danger of falling into the habit of overthinking. *Yes, I am reading too much into this. I should just keep quiet and enjoy this for what it was.*

However, I had to admit the obvious to myself. I liked her far more than I should considering the brevity of our acquaintance; her quiet manner, the simmering strength I saw behind the calm of her eyes. Everything about this girl served to make the possibility of loving her more real each day. I had made a promise to myself as well as to her the moment the realization hit me, that I would help her find her strength, as well as help her believe in herself.

"You're awfully quiet over there, Wyatt. Are you okay?"

It seemed as if she always brought me back from my thoughts, regardless if those were aimed at myself in disdain, or at her with wonder and gratitude. She always managed to make me forget my troubles, as well as the concerns that ran through in my mind. I would always be thankful to her for this. "I'm fine, Alex, there is no need to worry," I said, as calmly as possible.

"He thinks I can't tell..." she laughed to herself.

"Can't tell what?" I wondered as I peeked over from the edge of the page.

"When you're keeping something from me. I'm watching you, mister," she warned playfully, waving a finger at the book.

Could she really read me this easily? I asked myself.

"Yes, she can," answered the voice from 'the visitor', as I had come to think of it. "She is meant to be in your life, and so, she understands you. She might come to understand you better than you understand yourself."

"Well," I uttered, as disdain overtook the conversation. "You seem to think so."

"Wyatt, did I do something?"

I winced at the hurt in Alexandra's voice, my resentment obviously misplaced once I returned to my reality. "I'm sorry, Alexandra. I do not know what came over me."

She shook her head, dismissing my blunder, and laughed. "Calm down, Wyatt. I have pretty thick skin, you know? Besides, I know that you wouldn't say anything to hurt me intentionally."

I breathed a sigh of relief, and watched as her hair lifted slightly. *Was that me?* I thought to myself. What was happening?

"You are changing, Wyatt, and she is your catalyst," the voice whispered, and I felt my heart begin to speed.

"What do you mean that I am changing? What am I changing into?"

"You still have a long path ahead of you, don't you worry," it answered, cryptically.

"You know, if you are trying to be comforting, you need to work on your approach," I huffed. I felt the voice's laughter all around me.

"All will be as it should be, do not worry. I will leave you now."

I did not know why, but that last sentence sounded dark, as if danger surrounded the word's edges. I felt my skin prickle as my mind told me that something was not right with this, nothing at all.

"Wait, how are you so certain that Alexandra does not already know that you have contacted me? How do you know that she knows nothing of what you have told me?" My questions left her unaffected by the fear I was expecting, and she merely laughed.

"I've been here long enough to learn a thing or two about how to hide things," she smirked.

Chapter 5

Once again, Alexandra had fallen asleep, the book resting open beside her, so that I could guard her dreams. And guard them I did, as the glow of flames from the fire that she built every night brightened her face, which seemed to make her glow in the night. She was beautiful.

I would give anything to be able to touch you... I thought to myself as I rustled some of my pages, creating a soft breeze that swept her hair slightly.

"You could touch her," said from nowhere. "There will come a time when you will be able to be with her."

"How?" I wondered as excitement arose and escalated. "How would that even be possible? And how can you read my mind?"

"All in due time, Wyatt. You must be patient," she said in a lilting voice, and even though it spoke of trust, I could not help but feel wary.

I was about to reply when I heard a soft moan come from Alexandra.

"Looks like somebody's waking up," the voice said amused, "you might want to go to her."

I nodded and ran to the edge of the page, the short distance between me and Alexandra seeming to stretch on for miles instead of mere inches.

"Dad no! It's not my fault!" she yelled in her sleep, her figure curling in on itself while she shivered. It was almost as if she were trying to hide, her small hands forming into tight fists. "Wyatt!"

"Alexandra, wake up. You are dreaming," I whispered, trying to be as soothing as I could be. As her breathing suddenly stilled and she opened her eyes, I was expecting a quick brush off, similar to the last time this had happened, but was surprised to see tears welling in her eyes. "What is wrong?" I asked, and she trembled slightly, her eyes denoting the war raging within her.

Yet, despite her tumult she began to explain. "I just kept seeing my dad coming at me, and I was feeling panicky, but then you woke me up. In the dream, you stood between us, trying to keep him away from me, but he just pulled a knife from out of nowhere and stabbed you! And I just stood there watching as you fell in front of me, bleeding out, while dad looked shocked, but then laughed and said, 'You sure know how to pick 'em Lexy. Who'll protect you now?' Then he left, laughing as he walked away, and I was left with you dying in my arms," she rambled and ended with a shudder, her voice broken by unshed tears.

"That would never happen because I would not allow it," I said fiercely.

Alexandra laughed, disbelief coloring both her tone and her cheeks. "No? No offense Wyatt, but you can't exactly jump out of the book and protect me, can you?"

Her words stung because that was exactly what I wanted to do, but I could see in her eyes that they came from fear and stress stemming from her situation. Her breathing quickened, and she sniffled as the tears that had been hiding behind her sharp words began to overflow.

"Don't cry..." I tried to soothe, but then thought better of it. "No, I think you must cry to release all of that tension you carry."

She took in one big breath, and then released it. "I'm sorry, that was horrible of me. Uh, I'm fine. Don't worry."

I knew that she was lying, more to herself than to me, but I could also tell that she needed to stop the discussion. As did I. It was clear that talking about it was not going to help her at the moment, and that she would need time to find the strength to trust me. But I trusted that she would tell me when she felt that she could, or at least, I had no choice but to wait. Something was weighing on her, that much was obvious, but I knew that she had to be the one to decide to discuss her issues.

"I'm sorry I was so mean, Wyatt, I know you don't deserve it. I'm just really stressed," she said, giving me a sad look.

"Alexandra... I will worry, because I—" my breath caught, stopping short of my admission.

"Because you what, Wyatt?" she whispered, the smallest hint of annoyance in her tone.

"Because I have feelings for you," I admitted quietly, and her expression became frozen in surprise at my words, her breath stalled on an inhale. Shock engulfed me as I considered the fact that despite the fact that I felt as if I had been quite transparent, she still did not see how much I was beginning to care for her.

"H-how? Why?" she asked, incredulous, and I could not help but laugh in my disbelief.

"Please forgive my laughter, but I truly wish that you could see what I see when I look at you. I see someone who is caring, brave, strong, and resilient; so many wonderful things that make you the person that you are."

She blushed at my words, and I could not help ruffling a page to caress her cheek. That had become my favorite ability.

"And so beautiful."

She giggled sweetly at my touch, and it sounded like bells to my ears. "Well, you certainly know how to woo a girl, don't you? I... I wish you were real—well, flesh and blood, anyway."

Her admission seemed to heighten something within me, and if I had a heart, I imagine that it would be racing at the moment. Was it possible that she could ever feel the same way toward me? "Alexandra..."

"Nope, that was an embarrassing thing to say, and I don't want to add to my humiliation. So zip it," she ordered, running her joined thumb and forefinger across her lips.

"Alright!" I conceded, laughing.

"Good," she said, a satisfactory look on her face.

"All is well with us Alexandra, do not worry," I vowed.

She smiled in relief. "Thank you. You know, even though we hardly know each other, I can't help but think that you know me better than everyone I know."

Her words nearly made me blush. "I feel the same, Alexandra. I really do. You have made me come alive."

"I take it you mean that in the literal sense," she giggled.

"Indeed!" I exclaimed with a laugh, clearly enjoying our blossoming banter.

Alexandra came and went as she pleased, living her life in the outside world day to day, but always coming back to me at some point. Each day a new experience for us both. We spoke of her life, and with each passing day, it seemed that she became more and more comfortable with sharing, became more open with me, sharing details about herself and her life, albeit with some resistance. But for the most part she did not push me away. "Well, that's basically all there is to tell," she explained one day, after discussing her life further. She was a constant presence, and even as she left my side to be with her family, I felt as if she never really left my side. A constant presence. It was a comfort, even if I would always worry about her when she was not at my side. As well as a marker for time passing. Other markers were the refreshed glow she returned with, as if her spirit recharged every time. As well as the creek of the door opening as she let herself into the room. Days turned into weeks as we shared what felt like secret meetings between two lovers. We would always speak about her day, which she would elaborate on with an animated look on her face as she detailed the good as well as the bad. She rarely discussed her home life though. There was one day where she arrived with bags that she told me she would hide between the surrounding shelves.

"There will come a day when you will find yourself, Alexandra. When you will realize that you are so much more than you think you are."

A quiet smile played on her lips in response, which I counted as an improvement, a step up if you will, from where we had started. Once able to focus on her fully, I was able to note her appearance more effectively. Where she had seemed perfect to me before, now I was able to get a better understanding about her. As if she was allowing me to glimpse into her soul.

"What do you do when you're away?" I asked, all the while trying to make my voice sound a way that might be taken lightly. "What is your day like? You clearly know how I spend mine, so it is only fair that I get to know about yours."

Her mood shifted instantly from happiness to wariness. "Oh, you know, spend time with family, with my friends, and now with book characters. Regular teenage stuff." "What about school? You never really discuss it, and I never see you working or…" "Look, when I come here, the last thing I want to do is discuss my sad, everyday life. This place is filled with magic, and all you can focus on is my boring existence?" She sounded tense, clearly, maybe even angry

A thought came to me suddenly, darkening my previously good mood, and filling me with dread. "What do you think would happen if your father ever found you?"

She sighed, closing her eyes as she turned her face away from me. "I honestly don't know."

"I will never allow it," I seethed. "I promise you that."

"Take it easy, Wyatt. I'm fine, okay? He hasn't found me."

I nodded and vowed that he never would. Not if I could help it. *How would be able to do anything to help her? You are not exactly free to move as you please,* the thought filled me with annoyance and helplessness, and I felt a war raging inside of me, because I wanted to protect her. Because I would protect her.

But what could I do from this paper prison? Would I be able to protect her when I was trapped in here? Desperation simmered within me at the thought.

Chapter 6

What I wouldn't give to be able to touch you... I thought to myself as I looked at her. The look on her face was one that spoke of peace as she slept, despite everything she had been through. What I knew of, and what I did not.

"There will come a time when you will be able to be with her," said the entity with a voice from nowhere, recalling the memory of those words that persisted in my mind, the one that had given me hope for a future where Alexandra and I would find our path together. I could not see it clearly, and yet whenever I thought of that as a possible future, my heart sped and seemed to grow exponentially.

"Hey," she called to me, her voice heavy from sleep, breaking me out of my thoughts.

"Yes?" I replied, quickly.

"Are you okay? You seem a little... off."

I was amazed that she could sense my state of mind. I was, after all, not real. Could I be becoming like her? Tangible. A physical presence to be sensed? Something other than the whisper I considered myself. That would be impossible. Right? It seemed that the more time we spent together, the stronger the pull between us became. I was no longer just written word, and I could feel slight changes in me. It felt as if my heartbeat grew stronger day by day, and seemed to beat in time with hers, almost as if we were becoming one entity. I wondered if she felt it as well. When I looked at myself, I could also see a change taking place. Where I had not been able to see myself as more than a blur, now, I was able to discern my features more clearly. Still not with the sharpness of reality, but closer to something like it. "I am well, Alexandra. Just thinking, that is all."

Her brow furrowed as she tilted her head in response. "Well, don't get all quiet and moody on me. I'm a worrier by nature, so I will worry! Do you want to talk about it?"

"I am not sure that I should. Not yet anyway."

"Wow, is it that bad?"

"It is not, I promise."

"Alright. But for the record, you're a rotten liar," she said, looking at me with a smirk on her face.

The rustling came out of nowhere, one that was becoming all too familiar to me. As I mulled this over, I failed to see the fog that had encompassed my mind and created a barrier.

"Well, isn't she intuitive?" the voice mocked.

"What are you talking about?" I asked.

"Alexandra, of course, she already knows your quirks," she said with what sounded like a condescending laugh.

"How would you know that?"

"Oh, isn't it obvious? You know, I know a lot about you, Wyatt. You could say that we've known each other for quite a long time."

"How?" I insisted, and she seemed to hesitate before answering.

"I was there the day that you were created. Or would 'thought of' be a more accurate description? Sadly, toward the end, she became bored with you and left. She didn't complete you, obviously, but what she did was evidently enough. Such talent. After she left, the store became ghostly, abandoned. It was as if she had taken all sign of life with her."

"What happened to her?" My voice shook as my emotions turned erratic. Discussing my creator, the person that had abandoned me, was not what I had planned, but the lure of any revelation proved irresistible; even if the subject fanned my ire and resentment toward her and her abandonment.

"She just stopped coming around. She might have lost interest, I think," she said in a detached yet regretful tone, confirming my thoughts, and the words stung even though they were expected.

I thought back to when I had first realized what had happened, thought back to the fear that later turned to hurt, which was now turning into anger. I was abandoned. Discarded. Cast off as undesirable. What was once just a thought was now a solid, heart wrenching truth. "Stop. Just stop. I do not want to talk about that," I said, trying to restrain said anger.

"I am sorry. I wish I had known that it upset you to talk about this person," she apologized, her tone sympathetic.

"Wyatt..." I heard my name being called suddenly, as if from a distance, gaining worry as it kept calling. "Wyatt!"

"Alexandra?" I ventured, and out of nowhere came a great pull, seizing me from where I had been. I turned toward her, searching for Alexandra's beautiful gray eyes, to see that her expression was filled with panic.

"What happened to you?" she asked, her words high pitched and quick.

"I... do not know. I felt as if I was drifting off."

"But you were gone. I called and you wouldn't answer, I flipped the pages and couldn't find you. It was like you vanished," she explained, her voice seemingly calm, but I felt something brewing behind her timber.

"I am right here, and I am safe," I soothed.

"Well, don't do that again. Do you have any idea how scared I was!" she said, breath short.

What happened? I was right here, had been the entire time, right? I decided to mull this over later, because Alexandra needed me more. "Hey, I'm sorry I disappeared," I soothed, while trying to understand the situation myself, to grasp the thoughts that raged in my head, because I had no idea what that was. "I am here now. I am safe. Breathe for me, okay?"

"Don't do that to me," she whispered, clearly trying to calm herself. "You can't disappear on me again. Promise?"

"I promise," I said honestly.

"And I'm sorry for the outburst, things just got away from me for a second there. Not a good feeling," she excused herself with a nervous trickle to her voice.

"Are you really okay?" I asked, concerned. "That seemed…"

"A bit much, didn't it?" she sighed, "Sorry, I just felt a bit scared."

I spent the next couple of hours trying to explain what had happened to both her and myself, but when I tried to recall those events, it seemed as if I were trying to view objects through many veils. There was no clear evidence as to what happened to me in the time I was gone. The calm and gleeful demeanor she possessed appeared to have dissipated, dissolved into a quiet, anxious rage. It was enough to make me momentarily uneasy.

What happened? Why was Alexandra reacting this way? I had not gone anywhere. Had I? It was all a blur now, the conversation, the girl... My memories seemed to resemble grains of sand that slowly sifted through a sieve, but something told me to be careful, especially concerning the voice. As if I could not, should not, trust this voice; even though I did not know why. I chose to leave the situation for another time, not wanting to make any hasty accusations against the girl. Could she be lying about everything? Could she be trying to gain my trust to then use it against me or Alexandra?

I fell silent as the ache to touch Alexandra became a living entity within me, one which gained strength with each passing day. I could feel it drive me to reach out and run my hand soothingly along her arm. Would I feel that touch? Had I felt it previously? Try as I might, I could not recall. The disappointment of not being able to sense her skin made me want to cry. But that would not work, would it? I would still be left with the privation, the longing for that simple contact of my hand on her cheek. Thoughts of my conversation with the voice came back to me, thoughts of telling Alexandra about what was happening, and what was being offered to me.

"Alexandra?"

"Yeah?" she murmured, the remnants of sleep seeming to want to cling to her.

"Do people normally sleep that much?" I joked lightly, making her laugh.

"Well, I've been kind of busy entertaining you, haven't I? That takes up energy," she defended.

"Fair point. I need to talk to you," I said, thinking of how to explain what was going on.

"What's wrong? Are you okay?" she asked, concerned.

"I am, no need to worry. I just..." I then dove into the conversation, recounting all about the voice, and what it had told me. She

41

was quiet throughout, waiting patiently for me to finish, her expression becoming more worried by the minute.

"I don't know, Wyatt. I don't think I trust this," she said, her tone rife with concern.

My suspicions were not just my own anymore, which seemed to cement them further. "I am not sure that I do either. The last time we spoke, I felt strange, as if she was even more of a presence than before. I could feel her watching me, but I could not see her."

"Please be careful, Wyatt. Something about this doesn't feel right to me," she warned me. Seeming to drift off into her thoughts, she asked, "Do you think that she might be why you disappeared?"

"What do you mean?"

"Come on, we just talked about this," she said, smirking.

A sudden chill came over me. Did the voice have something to do with what happened? I did not know what to think, but I did know that this was further proof that the voice was not to be trusted.

"I had no idea, Alexandra. Please believe me."

"I do, I just... It was scary, not knowing where you were or what happened to you..." she explained, and there was a slight tremor to her words.

"You worried about me?" I asked as my heart increased in rhythm.

"Of course! You are my friend Wyatt, how could I not worry about you?" she said, steadfast, her eyes seeming to echo something to me. "You do know that if you ever needed my help, I would try my best to be there for you, don't you?"

"Yes, I do. And I am very thankful to you for that," I said, honestly.

"So, can I ask what it is that you do when you're bored? I'm just making conversation."

I laughed at her random train of thought. "Well, I mostly just walk around here, think about things. That type of stuff."

"What do you think about?" she asked, timidly.

"I think about you."

"Me?" she asked, confused.

"Yes, you. I think about the wonderful person you are, your beautiful heart, and your kindness. I just think about how everything about you is beautiful," I told her, feeling like a broken dam as speech spilled out of me in a rapid flow.

"Um, let's change the subject now, okay?" she said, blushing.

I felt a pang in my chest at this, but I knew that I would not give up because she had become too important to me. "What about you?" I asked, trying to gauge if I could find out more about her.

"Well, I think I pretty much moved in here. I can't necessarily go home because my dad—" Her words shut off instantly, stopping mid-sentence. The fear written all over her face at the mere mention of the man was enough to give me an idea as to what was going on.

"Your father hurt you," I concluded out loud and she nodded.

"I-I don't like talking about it. And before you say anything, no, I am not trying to let him off the hook, because I know what he's done. I just hadn't been able to get away until now. It's one of the reasons why my friend came barging in here last time, remember? She was... is worried about me."

I nodded in understanding. "I still think that you would benefit from discussing him; at least it would help you get something off your shoulders."

She captured her bottom lip between her teeth and cast her eyes on the worn carpeting. "I don't know..."

"Try," I encouraged. "I know you can do it. You can trust me."

She exhaled a shaking breath. "Okay. But if this in any way comes back to bite me, I will..." she threatened, trailing off with her mouth set, her eyes seeming deep in thought, "dog-ear your pages."

I winced. "You have nothing to worry about."

"Good."

"So, tell me about yourself. I think it's only fair to ask since you practically know everything about me," I said, an audible smirk to my tone.

"We've been over this, Wyatt. There's not much to tell," she retorted with a huff, turning away from me.

"You built a wall around yourself, Alexandra..."

"You think I don't know that?" she scoffed, her voice and temper escalating. "I have to keep this to myself because it is messed up and ultimately pathetic. I'm the girl that up until a few weeks ago couldn't leave her house except to go to school. My dad is a nightmare, zoned out on his best days and violent at his worst." She stopped suddenly, taking deep breaths to calm herself. "The days I've spent here have been like a vacation for me, times when I don't have to worry that my actions will trigger any violence. With a friend I never could have imagined—" she paused again, as if realizing that she may have said too much. "I'm sorry; I shouldn't have exploded like that."

"Don't apologize, Alexandra. I wish that you could see yourself the way that I do. You are such a strong, beautiful person."

"Well, I guess I don't share your vision."

"I truly wish that you did. You have gone through so much, and the fact that you are still here speaks volumes of your strength. The way that you can still see beauty all around you, as well as the way that you always see the best in any result, in every situation. You just have to learn to see that strength in yourself."

Tears sprung from her eyes at my words, and I wanted nothing more than to take down the walls that kept her from me. "I wish I could see myself like you do."

"You will, it seems it will take some time, but you will," I said, honestly.

"So now you know my secret. I'm a tortured soul..." she sighed, her voice coated in sarcasm.

"You do not have to be, Alexandra, you can be the strong person I know you are. You don't see yourself clearly at all."

"I'll get there, I'm sure of it. There are just a lot of things I need to work through, you know? My mom, my dad..." she said, playing with her fingers.

"I know, Alex, and I would love to help if you would let me," I said, trying to hide my anger at the mention of her progenitor; I would never go as far as calling that man a father.

She looked at me in earnest, her eyes shining as if tears were pooling and threatening to spill over, the frustration in her voice nearly palpable. "Ugh, I hate this! I'm such a wimp. I wish that I could get through this without crying at every turn."

"You are strong, Alexandra. I can see that, now you just have to see it for yourself. I imagine that few people could handle what you have had to manage in your life and be as resilient as you." I grazed a page along her cheek. "You are the person that you are thanks to everything you have gone through, and I l—" I stopped myself from revealing my secret because I doubted that this was the right time for her to hear it.

She stilled at my words, tears were streaming down her cheeks, and a wide-eyed look on her face. "Y-you, what?"

There was no way to hide it any longer, even if I wanted to. "I love you, Alexandra."

A violent wind seemed to arise from nowhere, pushing and pulling me, tossing and turning me in the air. It was wrenching me away from her and seemed to also be beating me senseless. Why could I sense a whisper of vengeance in it? I kept twisting and turning in the wild wind, grasping at nothing, a furious pounding like a caged animal in my chest. The stop came abruptly, the end of the turmoil seemed as sudden as its beginning. The only evidence of it ever occurring came in the form of a dizzying pain in my head.

"What happened? Where am I?" I groaned as I gripped my head, trying in vain to make the world stop spinning.

"Well, hello again, I think you might be a bit disoriented," said the all too familiar voice, and I blinked the shock from my eyes when I thought that I could hear a threat behind its pleasantry.

"Who are you?" I demanded.

"Have you forgotten about me so quickly? I am hurt..." the voice said sadly, and yet, I could sense a bit of mockery behind it.

"What have you done with Alexandra?" I asked, a slight agitation surfacing within me.

"She is fine," the voice said with a disinterested tone, "I just wanted to talk to you alone."

"And where is this happening, exactly? Where am I?"

"Oh, we're just hiding for a bit, that's all. Away from any listening ears."

My previous feelings of distrust and irritation began fighting the haze that had apparently overtaken me, making my speech brisk. "Well, I need to get back, so if you could kindly get on with it."

A resigned sigh sounded all around me, and all at once, I felt something akin to a slap on my cheek, and it left me reeling. It seemed to come from nowhere, but it left a searing trail all along my face. I looked on in shock, watching as the being materialized before me. Along with it, came a rapid gust, which increased its force almost immediately.

My hands began grasping at anything that might keep me grounded where I stood, futilely reaching out for anything that might anchor me, but my efforts were futile as I was swept up in its turmoil regardless. Anything that could have helped me appeared to dance out of my reach, as if it was all following her lead. I felt pressure coming from all sides, compacting me slowly, and pain seemed to emanate from within.

"Such a temper... Tsk. Tsk. You truly must learn to control it," she teased, and commanded the tumult to a pause. The thrashing stopped immediately, for which I was thankful, but I still felt unsteady. As if I were still drifting in the air. "I simply wanted to see how you were, and this is the attitude I receive? That is sad," she sighed, sadly.

"Get on with it, then," I hissed, angrily. A simultaneous tug and push from within making me feel ill and disoriented as I tried to fight against the surge, trying to regain as much as I could of the control I had gotten over myself.

"You seem to be becoming quite attached to the girl. She is pretty, I suppose," she said with disdain.

"If I am, that is no business of yours. And I would appreciate it if you showed some respect toward her," I said angrily. How was it that this being could make my temper flare so easily?

"Of course," she agreed, her tone taking on a sweet and docile quality, but there was also an edge to it.

My feelings of mistrust grew with each word she uttered, and I knew that I would no longer trust this being. Regardless of how inoffensive she seemed. I would not allow myself. And I had a sinking suspicion that she knew this.

As it usually occurred after I met with her, I was thrust back into Alexandra's world, which I had come to regard as my reality.

"You promised that you wouldn't disappear on me again, Wyatt. What happened?" Alexandra's voice broke me out of my thoughts.

I again had to calm Alexandra's worries upon returning, but if I was being honest with myself, the fact that this being could bring me to her side in an instant was not comforting in the slightest. This being was powerful; that much I could feel whenever I was with her.

"I do no—" I began, but decided against lying to her. I knew that I could trust her, that I should trust her. But for some reason, I could not help the reaction to steel myself. "It is a being that lives within the book. It—She likes to speak with me."

"You mean she likes to kidnap you! Do you remember me explaining how you disappear whenever you 'talk' with her? And not like, 'Oh, I'll be back in five minutes' either. You were gone for hours."

Those words, combined with Alexandra's reaction, cemented my earlier thoughts. I could not trust this being. I decided then to play things by ear, because I feared that if I displayed any changes in my demeanor toward this entity, things would take a turn for the worst, and that just could not be.

"Wyatt, I'm serious. Something about this doesn't seem right," she said with a tremble in her voice, hugging herself against a sudden and inexplicable chill that invaded the room. "Oof, why is it getting so cold in here?" she shivered.

"I do not know, but I feel it too," I said, as I felt my pages start to stiffen and become rough from the decrease in temperature. I felt my breathing become short, and an overall sickening feeling as this went on. I started to cough and gag, feeling sick.

"What's wrong?" Alexandra asked through chattering teeth, as she slowly broke away from the cold and focused on my voice. "Wyatt!!"

I heard her shout, but she sounded so far away. My eyes had closed involuntarily as if I had been lulled to sleep. I inhaled forcefully. "I-I can't..."

The next thing I knew, the world around me went blank, and I couldn't help but succumb.

"You don't belong with her," the voice called from a distance.

"You... What are you doing? Why are you doing this to me?" I forced the words past the ice wall barricading my throat.

"I've played nicely for too long, but I knew that I had to make you see," she explained, sounding as docile as water, but also as lethal as a tidal wave.

"I don't... Who are you? And... and why are you speaking differently all of a sudden?" I asked, suspicious.

"Silly Wyatt, can't you tell that there is a connection between us?" she asked, and her voice augmented as if she were leaning closer to me. "I know the one who created you," she said, her words obviously meant to caress, but instead seemed to cut through me like a thousand knives.

"W-who?" I stuttered as a sudden chill made me shiver.

"I will explain in time," she said, laughing, her voice pealing like bells. "You really did turn out nicely, I'll give her that."

"Thank you. Alexandra—" my mind answered and at the same time called out as if it were a desperate plea.

"That girl is nothing but a liar," she uttered in mild irritation. "She—"

"How dare you?" I interrupted. "All that you have done is lie. You say that you know who created me, but you want me to believe that my creator abandoned me! You have been watching me suffer all along, haven't you? And now, you insult the only person kind enough to help me, to care for me?" I ranted.

Anger had become a seed that grew in my heart, making my voice a physical force. I felt weightless, as if I was not really part of my shell anymore, and wanted so badly to return to Alexandra. As I thought of her, I felt a ripping within me, as well as around me, and on a whim, lifted myself off the page! I began to run away from her, feeling as if I were breaking free of chains.

Her expression seemed unfazed, but I could sense the warring ire and pain within her. "I couldn't stay! She—" her voice cut off suddenly in the midst of what felt like a confession. It sounded as if she were choking.

"Are you alright?" I asked, stopping in my tracks for some reason, bewildered as to why I was concerned with her well-being. But I was.

"She doesn't want me— talking— to you," she said, her voice breaking in between breaths. She sounded as if she were choking. "I- I can't. You have to go back— Go back to her," she said, in a broken whisper.

"Will you be alright?" Why did I care? I couldn't believe the concern that I felt for this being. But there it was, weighing down on my chest like bricks.

"I think so. Just go."

I heard Alexandra calling out to me again, and suddenly I felt myself being dragged to her side. I thought this meant my freedom; that I was allowed to live, and love, without having that constant shadow around me. But I was so far off...

Chapter 7

"Wyatt!" Alexandra's voice sounded as if from a distance, a beacon that guided me back from this blackness.

"Alexandra!" I called back as I ran without a clear destination in mind. Pain seemed to surround me, and I felt as if I was quite literally ripping myself in half, but I had to find my way back to her.

"You don't belong to her..." the entity echoed, and it sounded as if it came from nowhere.

"Yes, I do," I answered firmly. Almost stubbornly if I thought about it.

"No, you don't." Her voice became stronger, a phenomenon that I just could not ignore. There was something to it this time, however. Not anger, but sadness, a deep sadness that seemed to dig into me and permeate everything. Her words circled around in my head, as if she were there repeating everything she had said, trying to compound the message further.

Suddenly, the atmosphere around me became gloomy, the mood downright miserable. I could feel a deep pain cut right through me.

"She lies to you..." she said, her tone weaker than I had yet heard.

"Well, you lied too then," I replied angrily, steeling myself against the inexplicable hollowness I felt as I started to walk away.

"I only lied because s—" the voice was suddenly cut off, and I stopped as I became inexplicably worried all of a sudden.

But why should I be worried? This was the being that had kept me bound, was she not? She had gone as far as to try to hurt me, had she not! I should hate her! But now what I felt was confusion, as well as empathy for this poor creature. Clearly, this was plaguing my sanity.

"What is wrong?" I asked, suddenly worried.

"She doesn't want me talking to you. Not while she can't control me," she whispered in a strained voice. "I hate it when she does that."

"You have said that before. Why?" I felt a rise in temperature around me, and felt the resulting agitation as I heard my quickening breath. I glared at nothing, which only seemed to increase this feeling. I felt as if I were on the cusp of explosion.

"Because she doesn't want to be exposed. She doesn't want you to see that she is the evil one. Do you know how I felt when I had to say all those things? I felt violated, because all of it was forced," she said, her voice angry and bitter.

My mind rebelled against this. How could Alexandra be evil? That just wasn't possible. But something inside of me told me to listen, that I would regret it if I did not. "But how?" I asked, still trying to process this information.

"You might want to sit down for this..." she said, and when it became clear that I was not up for games, the voice took a deep breath, steeling herself. "This place wasn't always abandoned. Years ago it used to get a lot of visitors, and one of them was me. Everything started one day after I left school. I came in here because I was curious," she laughed, a mockery of a laugh, but it sounded pained nonetheless.

"Go on," I prompted, now curious despite my disbelief, and I felt her sigh.

"The place was busy, all except this one aisle for some reason. No one had went down it. If only I had known... I was looking at all the books, when all of a sudden I heard a voice calling to me. Now I can't bring myself to understand why I didn't run away, why I felt like I had to go near it."

"Near what?" I asked, even though I thought I knew her answer.

"Near this," she said with a flick of the pages. "I remember that I'd been coming here for a few days, when I started hearing something. At first I was scared, because I thought there was someone else in here with me. Now I know I wasn't wrong about that. As soon as I got close, I saw the book laying open on a reading stand. I know it sounds crazy, but I felt like the book was waiting for me. Well, I guess that's not so crazy considering everything that's happened." Her voice sounded deep in thought, as if she were miles away in her mind, but she seemed to come back to herself quickly enough after taking a breath.

"And that was when the book started sucking me in. It was so weird, because I felt like I was caught up in a storm. When I was able to focus on things around me, it looked as if everything was at a standstill. I screamed over and over, but no one heard me. All I could hear was a sinister laughter all around me, then everything went blank suddenly. When I woke up later, the witch was with me, and I somehow knew that she was more present in my body than I was. I guess she'd used the storm to take over my body, because all of a sudden, I was looking up at myself from a lower point. The numbness made me want to throw up, but that wouldn't have worked. Once she was in control of my body, she got access to everything. My memories, my emotions. Everything. I felt like I'd lost everything that made me myself. When I'd scream and call for help, she'd just tell me it was no use, that no one would hear me, and that I should preserve my energy. I wouldn't listen. I just kept screaming and trying my hardest to get noticed by someone. Anyone. But it was no use. I was trapped. That was when I realized that I'd been tricked. She'd made me think this place had been busy, made me see what she'd wanted me to see so that I would fall for everything, and I did. I cried for days after, for my family, for the life that had been taken from me, but then I became resigned to the fact that I was not getting out of here, and faded into the background. Once she had my body, she didn't need me anymore, but I don't understand why she didn't just kill me..."

She drifted off as desperation seemed to take her over like a shroud, but she quickly shook herself free of it. "Anyway, that was when she started working on her lover. I would see her write things out, and then I'd see things appear out of nowhere. I'll tell you, it was not for the squeamish." There was an abrupt pause from her, until she seemed to gather her thoughts. "Sorry, bad memories. Anyway, she would write him out with paragraph after paragraph, but never seemed satisfied. I'd see her writing from sunrise to sunset, and when she wrote, she would take on a different form. I didn't understand why. Soon though, she became bored with her design and didn't finish it."

"How do you know that?" I asked, curious.

"She took me along for the ride," she answered bitterly. "In the beginning, Alexandra thought that I couldn't be left alone because 'I still had some fight in me', so she dragged me everywhere with her. Much later, I started to notice that I'd lost interest in pretty much everything. Seeing everything and everyone I'd cared for move on, while I screamed for anyone to notice that the person they were seeing wasn't me. It broke me. She'd also take me on 'field trips' for inspiration."

Even as I felt her disgust, I didn't want to hear this. I tried to block it out, to make myself believe that she was lying. I could not help but realize the fact that this was sounding all too familiar. And I could not negate this being's experience. "So, you are trying to tell me that Alexandra was working on me," I surmised.

"Yes, she was," she answered in a tone filled with remorse. "She wanted to create a... 'beau'. 'If only you knew how lonely it can get,' she'd told me once. I'd dismissed the attempts at humor, because the fact that she would trap someone else made me sick. You have to stay away from her, Wyatt." Thoughts seemed to invade my mind in that moment, of how I felt as if my life revolved around her, as if I needed her to live. *Was I just a pawn to her? Some plaything to be manipulated at her whim?* Then I wondered why these thoughts were going through my head at all.

"How do you know all this? How exactly did she make you lie? Why should I believe you? You are the dishonest one in this scenario after all," I confronted suspiciously.

"According to her, right? Look, I know why you think that, and I don't blame you. But she was the one making me say those things. I promise. She tried to keep me hidden all this time too. But when you came along, I guess she became distracted, because I was able to break away. To answer your question about me knowing, I think she might have connected us at some point when she trapped me in here. How did she make me lie? She's had me in a tight grip, controlling everything. There wasn't much I could do without her knowing in the beginning. She'd make herself seem so innocent to everyone around us, while I was screaming to be heard. The only reason I've gotten away with as much as I have is because she's been so preoccupied with you. Whenever she'd speak through me, I'd feel like I wanted to throw up. I couldn't believe that so much evil could make itself seem so sweet and unassuming. And so convincing to everyone around her! Come on, Wyatt. Deep down you can feel that I'm telling the truth, can't you?" Her voice had turned supplicant, and as I mulled things over further.

I could not deny the truth that stared me in the face any longer, even though my mind was rebelling against it. My thoughts became erratic and my heart sunk, a deep sorrow weighing it down as if it were a solid entity. "I...." I sighed. "Even though it is hard for me to believe it, yes, I do feel that you are not lying to me. But then how—I mean, you yourself told me that she would help me. And she—"

"I thought that putting her on the spot and having you see what she was capable of would make it easier for you to believe me. That was all her. No one else could have done it."

"But she was so surprised that she could do it..." I kept hoping against hope that she was wrong, that I was not wrong about Alexandra.

"She's quite an actress," the voice mocked. "I've seen how she molds herself according to what she needs to manipulate and trap others. Keep them under her foot. She'll tell you whatever you want to hear, become whatever she needs to keep you. Answer me this then, why was she so keen on keeping you with her? Why would she freak out the way she did whenever you weren't at her beck and call?"

"I... I don't know how to answer to that," I admitted in shame. *Had Alexandra really taken me for such a fool?* I warred with the confusion and the heartbreak, as well as the anger that I had begun to feel. And I was losing.

"Wyatt, are you okay?" the voice asked, concerned.

I felt a light wind caress my cheek, trying to comfort me. "No! You want me to believe that the person I thought had saved me is also the one who abandoned me?" I asked, incredulous. "Do you expect me to believe you as if it were that simple?"

"I don't expect anything from you! I know what you must be feeling, Wyatt, trust me," she said, sounding on the verge of defeat.

"Really?" I uttered, sarcasm dripping from my tone.

"Yes, really. And while you're at it, you can cut the attitude. I'm not the one that trapped us here, after all, so I don't think I deserve it."

The reprimand was sharp, the voice behind it sounded ready to crack under the strain. And she was right. It did seem as though she was as trapped as I was, and maybe even worse, so her being responsible for all of this did not seem probable. Could it be possible that Alexandra truly was my jailer? I could not bring myself to think of that as a possibility. "I apologize. I just—"

"You're in love with her. Or you think you are," she sighed, defeat coating her words.

"Well, I—" I stopped as I came up short. I wanted so badly to defend Alexandra, my protests against these accusations just about to dive out of my mouth, but doubt seemed to hold them back. It became a material obstruction to any evidence I had wanted to present, and made it null in my mind. I wanted to defend my love for her, to brand it as genuine, but now it was becoming muddled, unclear, which led me to think that my feelings toward her were not as infallible as I thought they were. It was as if I had been blind, and had only recently been able to see some semblance of the truth. As if time away was clearing my mind.

"I do not know," I replied. And I truly did not know how to react to that. Were my feelings for Alexandra as fickle as this situation made them seem? Or was this the result of an underlying disappointment, a lie that she herself had fabricated for obscure reasons?

A thought dawned on me right then. Why had I not gone back to her? Alexandra always seemed to reach out to me when I was here before.

"Because I'm stronger now, so I can shield you." the voice replied with obvious pride.

"How did y—?"

"Haven't you noticed that I can read your mind?" she asked. "I don't know why, but I've been able to since the beginning."

That made me nervous, because I still did not trust this girl... witch... whatever she was, and I did not want her knowing my thoughts.

"I won't hurt you, you know. So you don't have to worry. I know it'll be a while before you can trust me though."

"Yes, it will. You—"

"That was all her. Not me. I don't expect you to believe me, but it's the truth," she defended, sounding as if she were on the verge of surrender. "She took everything from me, and I hate her for it."

I knew that she did. I could feel that hatred like air all around us, hot and restless, encased in a chamber, wanting so badly to find an outlet. "Hey now, let us calm down okay. Were you not telling me that you were not what you seemed?" I tried to soothe her.

"I was but people, like crystal, can only stand so much pressure before they shatter. And I'm near my breaking point with her. You have no idea what I've been through because of her. I've lost my friends, my family. Everyone!" she cried, her voice escalating to a crack, and I still could not believe that she could be talking about Alexandra. That just did not seem possible.

Chapter 8

"Stop, stop! I didn't say that I believed you, so stop——"

"But you do believe me. I can read you, remember? I know what you're thinking, and you're starting to doubt her, my friend."

I groaned in exasperation at her for making me face the thoughts that had been simmering in my head since she told me her story, and at myself for actually taking them for a possible reality. Was I starting to believe her? Had Alexandra really been the one to create me? Had she been lying to me the entire time I had known her? Had she taken the possibility of my wishes into account, or had she simply forged ahead, forcing her vision upon me?

"I'm sorry, that was stupid of me," the voice uttered apologetically. "But you frustrate me so much, you know? She's got her hands over your eyes, and it's like you're letting her keep you blind."

I could not defend myself in that moment, because I knew that it was true. I refused to face anything that might prove that Alexandra was anything other than what I knew her to be. And yet, I had a sinking feeling that the words were evidence that I could not ignore, regardless of how painful it was. Alexandra had lied to me. She was the one who had abandoned me, had led me to believe that I was alone for her own pleasure.

I was her plaything.

"Wyatt, can you say something, please?" the voice asked, subdued, but I was too consumed in my thoughts to answer.

Had Alexandra truly fooled me? Had she toyed with my trust? My world seemed to have shifted with each revelation, tilted on an axis that no longer seemed to be holding it in place. I felt betrayed, and what was worse was that I knew that the largest betrayal had been committed by me. I had betrayed myself in trusting too much. And yet, this felt different, as if the voice's words were a rock solid foundation that I could stand on; my trust in her becoming innate.

"What do you look like?"

"Are you sure you really want to know? Because I don't think you'll like the answer," she replied, wariness clouding her voice.

"Why would I not like the answer?"

"Okay, you asked for it," she sighed resolutely, and then proceeded to describe her appearance, which seemed to be an exact copy of what Alexandra looked like.

"I knew it! You have been trying to trick me!" I burst out, feeling betrayed for some reason.

"No! Wyatt, she took my body when she trapped me in here! Please! You have to believe me!" she cried frantically, her playful demeanor gone. Why could I not get past this point? It felt as if something kept me from seeing any other option.

"So everything that she told me about her father... Your father..." I drifted off.

She sighed, and I could sense her anger, as well as her sadness behind it. She laughed, incredulous. "That was true. Figures she'd use those aspects of my life for her act."

"I do not know why, but I believe you."

"Good." She sighed with relief, her voice carrying in the wind.

"You are smiling, I can hear it in your voice," I said, amused, and I realized then that I liked the sound.

"Yes, I am Mr. Smartypants." She giggled

I could not help noticing how similar she and Alexandra were, not just in tone, but also in manner, almost as if they were exact copies of one another. My heart was struck with pangs as I thought of how Alexandra had played me for a fool. "While we are discussing pleasantries, I do not think you have told me your name," I said conversationally as a means of distraction.

"Oh, so you trust me now?" she asked, aiming for sarcasm, but I could detect a bit of hesitant hope in her voice as well.

"And what if I do?" I asked, knowing that I was teetering over a dangerous edge.

"My name is Emily," she sighed, making me smile without understanding why.

The atmosphere around us shifted drastically then as anger became something tangible in the air. I felt a great pull that seemed to come from nowhere, and was almost violent in its force. I started to reach for anything, but nothing appeared to keep me from being extricated. Something managed to anchor me enough to keep me steady in the maelstrom, and even though I was still within the tumult, I had a better grip on my bearings. Something made the atmosphere around me thicker, making it possible for me to fix my position. And suddenly, the thickness materialized into a rope that I could use, as if changing to fit whatever I needed.

"Wyatt!" Alexandra's call came as if from a distance,

For the first time, I felt torn about answering her. Emily's story was still fresh in my mind and filling me with doubt. "What is happening?!" I yelled over the maelstrom.

"She knows you're here!" Emily shouted back. "You have to go back!"

"But I don't know how to get back to you!" I replied. And if I were honest with myself in that moment, I didn't know if I wanted to go back to her.

"Let her take you with her! It's the only way she'll stop this. You have to trust me!"

I nodded and closed my eyes as I released my hold, surrendering to this force, my mind's rebellion keeping strong regardless. I was tossed and turned, this way and that, all the while feeling rage and sadness envelope me.

"*Alexandra, I know it is you, and you know that I will go willingly. Stop this,*" I thought out to her.

The tumult calmed almost immediately, its previous anger being replaced by smugness.

"Well, that took you long enough to figure out, didn't it?" The figure that I had come to know as Alexandra appeared before me almost instantly, standing directly in front of me so as to have my undivided attention, and her tone was mocking.

"Yes, I guess I was blinded," I admitted, my double meaning not so well hidden.

"Aw, don't feel bad. You were merely following the path that I set out for you," she said with a smile.

"How could you? How could you deceive me like that?! H-how could you make me believe that I had been left alone! I trusted you blindly!" I was breathing hard, succumbing to a rage that I had no idea was building inside of me.

"I created what I wanted," she said, shrugging her—Emily's shoulders. "How many can say they have not wished for that?"

"I didn't!" I yelled. I was seething.

She laughed mockingly, and disappeared in an instant, only to reappear right next to me. "You really shouldn't look to make me angry, Wyatt. You have no idea who you're dealing with." Her tone danced between sweet and menacing as she played with the collar of my shirt. She leaned in, gripping my garment, and then her lips began to descend upon mine. I tried as hard as I could to get away, but it was as if she held me there by some unseen force. Some gravitational pull that refused to release me. I felt as if I were fixed into place.

The next thing I knew, her lips were on mine and my lungs were being robbed of oxygen. As the world fell away, darkness and emptiness overtook my heart. My world became devoid of hope, and nothing appeared to matter anymore. It felt as if I were fixed in that moment, unable to care about what was happening to me.

Was it her keeping me in this state? Or was it me? Had I really given up so easily? Then I thought of Emily, of how she was sharing my fate by being trapped in what to her was a non-world.

She had known freedom before this, and wanted to go back to it. And I knew that I could not give up, because I understood that her life was at stake as well. I did not care about what happened to me, but I did care about what happened to her. "No!" I cried, and somehow found the strength to fight off these symptoms. "I am not your puppet."

"Oh, but don't you see? You were never a puppet to me. You were always mine, as you always will be," she taunted, and removed herself from my presence, reappearing on the outside seconds later and walking away with a teasing wave.

Returning to Emily this time felt like waking from a deep sleep, the only difference being that I felt incredible pain.

"I will fight you," I vowed silently, and then turned my attention to Emily. "Well, it seems like I finally found a negative to having a body," I remarked with a wince.

"Are you okay? Wait, that's a dumb question. Of course you're not," Emily rambled, and I could not believe how much I had missed the way it made me laugh.

Until I hissed from the pain in my ribs. Alexandra had clearly used her time to hurt me without my noticing. The thought that she could do that was terrifying. "She's not too happy with me, I think."

"Makes sense," she said, lightly, and then her mood shifted to despair. "What are we going to do Wyatt? We can't just wait for her to go on a rampage and come after you."

"Or you," I added, because I had a feeling that Alexandra wouldn't stop at just one of us.

"Well, the way I see it, we have two options. We can either stay here stuck between these pages and wait for her to retaliate, or we can try to find a way out."

"Are you sure, Emily?"

"Yes, I am."

I felt sudden pride toward her as her once complacent and docile demeanor had given way to someone who was willing to search for her freedom, which in turn made me believe that I could aspire to it as well.

Chapter 9

"So... how are we supposed to do this, exactly?" Emily asked, her voice teetering between mocking and nervous.

I saw glimmers of a scared girl behind that playful mockery, one that was hiding behind a veil of annoyance. As I thought about it, I saw few options other than confronting Alexandra, but I didn't yet to know how to do that.

"We will figure something out," she said, feigning confidence.

Suddenly she cried out in pain, a searing pain that I could feel as my own. It felt as if I were being roasted from the inside, and I saw how she fell into a static state, and began to fade away from me. It happened so quickly that I did not know how, or if I could help her.

Anger began coursing through me, billowing like smoke clouds that threatened to choke me if I did nothing to release it. "Alexandra, stop! I won't let you hurt Emily anymore. Your fight is with me!"

"Such gallantry! Standing up for the damsel in distress," she cooed, her voice sounding all around me.

"What do you want, witch?" I asked, seething.

"Tsk, tsk, is that really any way to communicate with someone? I thought you had better manners."

"You leave me here, alone, and you expect me to be cordial?" I asked, incredulous.

"Cordiality is trivial to me. Respect is the least you could give. You would not exist without me, after all," she said haughtily.

"What did you do with Emily?"

"Oh, poor thing, I should be grateful to her for allowing me to use her body. Things would have been pretty uncomfortable in here if she had stayed as well, don't you think? But as you can see, everything worked out for the best," she laughed.

Allowing! "Emily did not *allow* you to usurp her. You took her body and trapped her in this book. You would have killed if you had not been so engrossed with her life!"

Anger rose inside me as heat radiated from my chest to the tips of my fingers before I felt it reach my eyes and make them shine with its glow. Her silver eyes began drawing me in, as if she were the flame and I the moth, and she was pulling me toward my end.

"No!" I yelled. "I know what you're doing, and I won't let you mislead me anymore. What. Have. You. Done. With. Emily?"

"You really should calm down, Wyatt," she soothed, her eyes seemed to concentrate their hue to look like molten silver. Through them came an invisible fire that seeped into me, burning me. I writhed in pain, remembering her choice punishment for me as the pain seemed to take over everything. Filling me. Surrounding me.

"Wyatt! Stop thinking. Just let your mind drift. It's the only way to get away from her," Emily yelled past the turmoil that ravaged my thoughts.

As I had done before, I let everything go; my worries, my confusion, my anger and frustration. I felt like liquid as I fell through my captor's hands with ease, to an unknown oblivion.

"That's it," she eased. "Relax. Come to me."

"Where are you, Emily?" I asked, my heart pounding like a hammer in my chest.

"I'm here. You're alright," she soothed.

"I thought she had hurt you!" I yelled as my anger escalated, and I could feel the tension from the previous altercation growing inside of me too. I wanted nothing more than to take her in my arms at that moment and for her to know that she was alright. That feeling was stronger now than ever before. The possibility of losing her struck a fear in me so strong that I could barely breathe. The moment I saw her again, just knowing that she was safe, felt like weights being lifted off.

"Shh, I'm here. I'm alright," she soothed.

"I wish that I could hold you," I said, before I could catch myself, and the atmosphere around us instantly become strained.

"You can't." Her voice held such sadness and frustration that it seemed to cut through me.

She was right though. Alexandra held us both captive in the worst kind of prison, and she seemed to delight in that fact. We had to think of a plan, a means of escape, but what?

"Wait!" she exclaimed suddenly, breaking me out of my thoughts. "What if we give her what she wants?"

"Are you insane?" I asked, near panic.

"Just listen to me, okay?"

Taking a deep breath, I settled down enough to hear this out, albeit with some apprehension. "Alright, tell me..."

"You can make her believe that you're in love with her, that you're ready to bend to her will and all that. Meanwhile, you gain her trust, learn her weaknesses, and then, we might just have a chance of getting out of here."

"I don't know about that."

"Oh, come on, she obviously wants you to love her. It would definitely work!" she said, and I could not help but detect a slight manic tone to her voice.

"Emily, are you alright? You are beginning to sound a bit..." I drifted off, getting the feeling that something might be wrong with her, but she seemed to catch herself and began to inhale slowly.

"Yeah, I'm alright. I think my being here for so long is start-ing to get to me though," she said sheepishly.

"How long have you been in here, exactly?" This was the question I had been curious about for a while, but always kept quiet, because I did not want to cause her pain. She went silent for one minute, two, three... I was about to resign myself to the fact that she would not answer, and tell her to forget about it when—

"I don't remember anymore, but it feels like I've been trapped in here forever...." Her voice sounded as if it were crawling through hot coals from the pain it emitted, and her admission cut through the last of my blind adoration for Alexandra.

I did not care about what she had done to me, that simply did not seem to matter anymore, but I did hate her for what she had done to Emily, for trapping her here, for taking her away from her family, all for no reason. I could understand her wanting to keep me here, but I could not fathom why she wanted to keep Emily. What reason could she have for that? This, above everything else was what made me hate her.

"I'm sorry," I said, feeling the need to apologize, but those two words felt wholly insufficient for all the pain that she must have endured.

"It's not your fault. She has you trapped here too," she said, her voice filling with tears.

"But you have a family, people that must be out of their minds with worry about you," I reasoned.

"They don't even know I am gone," she scoffed. And in that scoff I sensed her pain again, hidden under disdain. "When she trapped me here, she took my body and has been playing the part of the perfect daughter, the perfect friend; nobody even notices that it's not me."

I fell silent, unable to think of anything to say that might help to soothe her, no matter how hard I tried to think of something.

"It's okay," she exhaled. "I'm okay. I just lost it there for a minute."

I could tell she was waging a battle with her sanity, one that she was beginning to lose. The sadness and guilt over her family, the anger toward our captor for having stolen her life from her, everything seemed to be taking its toll on her. I knew that it was valid, but I wanted so much to keep her heart untainted by hatred. But what could I say? What could I do when I was as stuck as she was?

"I just wish that for once, they could see past her little act. That they could have realized that it wasn't me in there, you know? But that would lead to trips to the psychiatric ward, most likely..."

"Well, at least it wouldn't be you that would be going," I joked, trying to lighten the mood.

"No," she giggled quietly, her mood shifting slightly. "I guess it wouldn't be me."

"There's my girl!" I cheered, and immediately backpedaled. "Uh..."

She giggled quietly. "Wow, a flustered Wyatt. Nice."

As I thought about it again, I felt confusion and happiness at the same time. Confusion, because I had felt this way before, but that confusion was aimed toward Alexandra, which I thought I would never feel. Happiness, because I did feel it, and was sure of the person it was directed toward. Fear mixed in as well as I thought that it might have come on too fast, and I did not want to scare her. I was scared enough for the both of us, but I could not deny it, I was falling in love with Emily.

"I've been meaning to thank you, by the way," she commented, unknowingly interrupting my realizations.

"For what?" I asked, distracted.

"For what you said about my dad," she smirked, and I had think back a bit, but was finally able to pinpoint the conversation she was referring to.

"Oh, I..." I swallowed my sudden bout of nerves. "That was real?"

"Yeah, I keep that to myself, but Alexandra likes to play the tape for viewing audiences," she scoffed, and I could not help the ache that I felt in my heart for her.

"You're welcome," I offered sincerely, and hoped that she could hear the apology in my tone.

Chapter 10

As the days turned to weeks, a realization struck me to my core. I was falling in love with Emily, and it clearly was not coming along as my feelings for Alexandra had, which only served to prove that those hadn't been real. This was a slow burning candle that consumed me with emotion.

"Emily, I—" I stopped talking, unsure of her reaction.

"Yeah?" she asked, concern lacing her tone.

I loved that she always worried about me. I loved that she made me laugh, even when I thought that laughter was beyond me. I loved... her.

She looked at me, her eyes wide and full of emotions that I could not decipher.

"I love you," I declared, revealing my truth to her.

"You don't mean that," she said, her voice expressing a deep sadness. "You're still in love with her."

"I do mean it," I said, trying to suppress my emotions, which were in turmoil. "Those feelings are gone now. You did that, Emily." I hoped that she would believe me, but I could see that it was going to take some time for her to believe it.

She started retreating then, feeling farther away with every second that ticked by.

"Don't go! Please..." I begged.

"It's not me, it's her. She found you, and she's pulling you away." Her voice sounded farther away with every word she said.

"Emily!" I cried out.

"Don't fight it. Go to her. It'll be worse if you don't," she advised, her voice emotionless.

Behind it however, I could hear her defeat, which worried me so much more. "Em, please don't give up. Keep fighting," I urged as I felt the pull again and reluctantly gave in. "I love you."

I knew that I was back in Alexandra's presence when I felt an immediate blow to my chest that made it impossible for me to breathe, my torturer making herself known almost instantly.

"How nice to see you, Wyatt!" she burst out with a deceitful warmth.

"I cannot say the same," I replied, feeling strained.

"But why not?" she gasped, her voice feigning sadness. "I thought we were past that little rough patch."

"Rough patch? How can you call that a rough patch?! You could have hurt—" I stopped, afraid that my concern for Emily would be made more obvious if I continued.

"Oh, you shouldn't worry. I wouldn't hurt her, Wyatt," she cooed threateningly. "Not unless you gave me reason to."

"I wouldn't," I said, silently gritting my teeth.

"Good," she said, apparently appeased, showcasing a twisted smile that had no business being on Emily's face, a smile that seemed to root me in place and rob me of breath. Noticing my difficulty, her mood shifted slightly to worry. "Are you alright?" she asked in a concerned yet knowing tone

I felt my chest constrict, intensifying my need to breathe as I tried to find my grip, but was unable to find purchase.

"Oh, I know!"

Suddenly I felt a forced pressure on my lips, as well as a lessening of the one in my chest. My lungs were finally able to retrieve the air they so desperately needed.

"That's better, isn't it?" Her question was cheerful, as if she hadn't just tried to suffocate me. Again.

"W-Why?!" I shouted hoarsely, the air coming through what I felt was a corroded pipe, burning its way through the metal.

"Because you should learn by now that I am the only one meant for you. Not that specter," she replied in a derogatory tone.

Emily is more to me, than you'll ever be, I thought as heat roiled inside me, and anger surged with it.

Her anger radiated from her now, a white hot flame that sought to engulf everything in its path. I did not care, because I'd had enough. I was tired of hiding, tired of hurting, of feeling like her puppet.

"You may have created me, but you left me. You then tortured me for the sake of your amusement. That is not love."

"How could you know what love is?" she laughed.

"Because you wanted me to love you, did you not? You started to teach me, did you not? But you were unable to. I thought that I loved you, but I know that was just an obsession. I know that I love Emily!" I shouted, paying no mind to any possible repercussions, because I was tired of hiding my true feelings.

Alexandra laughed, the sound grating to my ears, where it had once sounded like music. "The book girl? You dolt, you will never be together as long as you're here. And since you can't escape me, well that just puts a damper on your little crush, doesn't it? You might as well surrender and give yourself over to me now," she said flippantly.

I knew that I needed to think of something, anything that could help Emily. But what? "What about a trade?" I proposed.

"What could you possibly have that would be worth a trade? I made you, after all. Without me you have nothing," she taunted.

I knew that I had to think quickly of anything that she could want badly enough to barter our freedom with. As I thought of the solution, I realized that only one of us would be released, but that was a sacrifice that I was willing to make. "Me," I answered, resolutely. "I will stay behind if you let Emily go."

At my reply, I felt a flare of anger, which faded almost instantaneously, and was replaced by amusement. "You are ever the valiant gentleman, aren't you? So willing to sacrifice yourself for your friend," she said with an amused, yet mocking tone, and I knew that I had to focus, because I would not be bated.

"If you release Emily, I will stay here forever."

Out of nowhere came a sound like ripping, as if someone was actually destroying a piece of fabric. *Wyatt, no! What are you doing?* Emily called to me, her voice resonating.

I'm trying to help you, I thought to her.

Are you crazy?! If she catches you... Clearly you need me to reign in your idiocy! Please don't do this. She'll just twist everything for her advantage, she said in warning.

"Well, well, look who's here," Alexandra chimed in. "I thought you would have vanished by now, girl. It doesn't matter though, you will eventually. You really thought you could hide from me? You're not capable of it."

"I've been able to keep you away," Emily defended, her voice rigid.

"Not well enough," Alexandra laughed. "I could still hear you, faintly of course, but clear enough.

As I listened, I could not help but be filled with rage at this exchange. "Leave. Her. Alone." I fumed, punctuating each word with the hatred I felt toward her; at which point, I felt the stares of both focus on me. Emily's was filled with disbelief, admiration, and... love? Was that really love I felt coming from her? I hoped it was.

Alexandra's voice, in contrast, was filled with a searing anger. Her scream followed seconds later, and seemed to shatter the world as I had come to know it. Everything that she had created for me started to crumble around us. The walls shook and rattled, debris raining down like a waterfall as groans and creaks gained momentum. The downfall would not take long.

"Why are you doing this?" I shouted in the midst of the maelstrom.

"Because I created you. You belong to me. You are meant to love *me*, not to fall in love with her!" she shouted, blasting everything into darkness.

All around me, there was this bleak and aggressive silence, nothing around me except for the bitter memories and the echoes of the loneliness I had felt before Emily appeared.

"No! I don't belong to you! You may have created me, but that does not mean that you own me!" I yelled, and thrust my arms out, pushing against her with everything that I had. It was like pushing against a wall, as if all the effort in the world would not be enough to make it budge.

"Wyatt!" Emily cried out in warning.

"No, Emily! I will not let her ruin our lives anymore," I said, defending my stance, and turned toward the source of my anger. "You say you love me, but love doesn't mean keeping someone caged in."

"I suppose you think it will be easy to get rid of me?" Alexandra questioned, her voice filled with dark amusement. "You belong to me."

"No, I don't! You left me alone and scared out of my mind. And now you have the gall to say that you own me? No, you do not own me. I want nothing to do with you!"

Her ensuing rage blasted me with smoke and left me rooted where I stood. As it burned me alive, scorched me from the inside out, I was powerless to stop it. "Emily, I'm sorry," I thought, as defeat overwhelmed me. "I love you."

The words ran through my mind and the flames erupted and grew stronger by the minute, as if Alexandra was punishing me for not succumbing to her. When I felt her gloating satisfaction brought on by my pain, I hated her even more, which I thought was impossible at this point.

"I'm so sorry, Wyatt. I love you too," came Emily's pain-filled response.

At her words, the fear of losing her became all consuming, and shook me to my core. I pushed again as her voice seemed to renew my strength, and could feel the wall giving away under the force I exerted. I now had the strength to fight her. "Don't you dare give up, Emily. I will not lose you!"

Suddenly, that all-consuming fire was doused and replaced by energy equal to its strength, surging from an unknown point and flowing inside me. My limbs vibrated with its hum. I looked to my surroundings, everything seemed to glow. No. It wasn't my surroundings. It was me.

Chapter 11

The violent vibration began to slow, dangerously so, making breathing difficult and made me clutch my chest. Out of nowhere, it stopped as quickly as it had begun.

I could no longer feel my heart, or hear it beating inside of me. I collapsed, reaching for anything that might possibly help me, even though I knew there was nothing there. It was then that I felt a light patter come from my chest.

Was I dying? No, not dying... I was very much alive. *Real.* Where I had once been disembodied, I now had substance. Well, an outline of myself anyway. *I'm real!* As I slowly came to terms with that fact, that patter turned into an energy filled vibration, which built up inside me, and coursed through my veins. There went my heart again, making its presence known by the loud, rhythmic thumping in my ears. *What is happening to me?* The shaking persisted to the point where I didn't know if it would ever stop.

"Wyatt..." came Emily's voice in my head.

I immediately looked around, frantic in my need to find her, but I couldn't see her anywhere. "Where are you, Emily?"

I had to admit that it was my bubbling curiosity, as well as my need to find her, that compelled me to move. I lifted myself, not knowing what I was expecting. Dizziness took over, but as I looked at myself, I saw that I had slightly come off my pages. I tried to loosen myself further, and found that I was successful.

How was this possible? I could feel something else now too, something sharp that pricked at my skin. Just as I had always imagined electricity would feel like. Maybe... Could I have Alexandra's powers? No, that could not be possible... Could it? How?

"How indeed?" Alexandra asked in a menacing whisper. "You really do seem to have acquired some of my magic, my love."

"What does that mean?" I asked, feeling something foul coil in my stomach at the sound of her voice.

"It signifies carelessness on my part, really, because I didn't shield myself when I was creating you. I thought that I could trust you! Oh well, not to worry. All will be as it should be soon enough. Hold on one moment, would you, darling?"

All around me stilled suddenly, while the air felt as if it was weighing me down. Alexandra appeared in front of me. She no longer hid behind Emily's face, but I had no way of knowing if this raven haired figure was truly hers. As she looked at me, her crystalline eyes were alight with purpose as I began to feel a pull from within myself.

One which I fought against as much as possible. "What are you doing to me!"

"Oh, hush. I'm only trying to give you a gift," she said, placidly. "But I need my magic to do it, and since you were born of that magic..."

"W-what are you doing?" I asked, my voice trembled involuntarily as she reached in front of me.

"Shh. Watch."

As I looked on, a faded figure seemed to appear in front of me, a body that lay motionless.

"I must say that I made a good decision on this. He really does suit you," she said approvingly as she ran her eyes over the figure, and then turned to look over at me. "Come closer."

When I refused to move, she was the one to advance. Not toward me, but toward the shell. Her hands roamed his chest, and as her lips descended upon his, I noted that I was experiencing the sensations that corresponded with her touch on the physical form. The pull seemed too strong for me to resist.

Within seconds of the kiss, I felt the fire raging within me, while the body appeared completely unaffected.

She released me in an instant, bringing about a relief so great that tears spilled from my eyes.

"This is you, my love," she cooed, proudly.

I knew that her love for me was toxic and torturous, that she was toxic and torturous, but I had no idea of what I could do to escape her.

"Where is she? What did you do to her?" I asked, my voice teetered between confusion about what I was seeing and my worry for Emily.

"Why must you always assume that I did something to her? Wouldn't it be just as easy to believe that she just disappeared?" she asked, her voice sounded breathy, weaker somehow. She seemed to be faded somehow, as the air around us filled with sounds of gasping.

What was happening?

"Never," I seethed. "Emily would never leave me willingly. Where is she?"

"Well, if you must know," she answered, gasping. "I haven't found her. Not that I haven't been trying, mind you. Yet, I don't know where she is." Her voice did little to mask a frustration that was clearly trying to claw its way to freedom.

A warm breeze blew around me then, bringing me to my knees with the strength of the hope it brought me. "She's alive, I know it. She has to be. Please let her be alive," I prayed, and when I finally did feel her presence, I gained a renewed strength to keep fighting Alexandra, searching not only for my freedom, but for Emily's freedom as well.

"If I have my way, you will never get your hands on her," I said, my protective instinct at full force. I would do anything I possibly could to keep Emily safe.

Alexandra laughed, challenging me. "That is cute. I must tell you though, that I can no longer be gentle with you, Wyatt. You simply seem to refuse anything I offer, and that includes your safety. You really are hurting my feelings. I had hoped that you'd changed your mind and realized that pleasing me was your best alternative. What a pity...."

"Like hell," Came Emily's voice, fragile but present nonetheless.

Hope filled me at the sound, and my heart began to beat in double time when I realized that she was alright. "*Emily...*" my voice trailed off as my heart filled with a relief so strong that it nearly sent me to my knees. Everything inside of me felt about to collapse from relief.

"Wyatt..." Emily called out to me.

"Emily!" I called back, wishing for the nth time that I could hold her in my arms. "Are you alright?"

"I feel like I've been run over by a truck," she said, her voice weak.

I couldn't help but linger on that sound as my mind drifted to the worst possible thought, but I reprimanded myself almost instantly, and quickly returned my attention to her.

"Do you know what she did to you? Because you just disappeared, and when I could not find you, I just about went crazy."

"I could feel you," she said sadly. "I wanted to reach out to you, but I couldn't."

"All is well, Emily. I am here now, and you are safe. Do you hear me? That is all that matters," I soothed, my voice shaking as I released a breath. She truly was the balm to my emotions, the calm to my storm. As long as she was with me, I felt like I could face anything. A sound of ripping erupted suddenly, loud and lengthened, and clearly meant as a distraction. Soon after it, I felt that ripping deep within me, as if Alexandra were tearing my body apart. The sound that emanated from me seemed alien, as well as excruciatingly pained, and I was rendered a crumbled, writhing mess because of it.

"Oh, I'm sorry. I didn't mean to disturb this happy reunion, but I have been so anxious to find you, Emily," Alexandra said with disdain, as she caught Emily in her grasp.

"Let me go!" Emily shouted as she tried to force herself away from our captor.

"You have been very difficult to find, haven't you," Alexandra stated.

When I heard Emily's struggle, I looked to see her slowly appear in front of me, a clear entity slowly made visible by Alexandra's touch. "You already took my body and my life. What more do you want?!"

"And I thank you so much for it. This really has been quite an experience, but I can't have you charming Wyatt. You'll just distract him, and I can't have that," Alexandra said, feigning kindness, and Emily began to choke. Her breath became ragged and short.

I could feel her affliction as if it were happening to me, the shortness of breath, the pressure at my neck and chest. We were both being assaulted, but I knew that there were different intentions behind both of these attacks. Where Alexandra merely meant to punish me, she sought Emily's death outright.

"I have had enough of you, Alexandra. Let her go! I do not love you and I never will! I love Emily!" I yelled, and then felt like I was hit in the stomach, as if I were slammed in the gut with great force, but I knew it was her rage that was now beating me to within an inch of unconsciousness.

"All of this could have been avoided, you know? You were meant to love me! We would have been so happy!" Her voice became shrill with the frustration that she tried so hard to keep hidden.

"And what about Emily? Would you have left her trapped here? All for the sake of a body? What next? Were you planning on trapping someone for me too?" I demanded.

"That was going to be my next task, but I decided that it would be less complicated to create one," she said, matter of fact like. "Won't it be wonderful?"

Her excitement over this plan enraged me, but as an idea started to break through my thoughts, I felt a spark of hope.

"Then you could create a body for yourself."

Alexandra tilted her head, and looked at me as if she was truly considering my suggestion, while she stroked Emily's arm lovingly. "Why would I do that, Wyatt? I've already spent so much time with this one. And it is the body you fell in love with."

"You are sick! Do you know that?" Emily snapped, her voice escalating as she struggled against the binds that Alexandra had put on her.

"No, I am simply someone who pursues their happiness at any cost. I wanted to be free of this paper prison, so I endeavored to find a viable escape. I wanted a companion, and I created one, even if I might have to make some adjustments. But mark my words, he will be mine. And I will dispose of any obstacles that get in the way of that," Alexandra seethed, her control nearly gone.

"If you think that I will let you get your hands on her..." I threatened, my anger climbing at a dangerous pace once again.

"Oh, but don't you see Wyatt? When it became obvious that you were straying, I devised to take your will away," she said, her tone amiable and sweet to the point of sickness.

It was at that point that I felt it. The wind, subtle in its potency, but cold as ice, a freeze that had come on only to encase me. And regardless of how hard I tried, I could not move a muscle as the icy vapors seeped into me and creep along my body, before finally disappearing as if they had not existed at all. But I did feel their effects on me, the numbing of my limbs, as well as my ragged, failing breath, and I knew that my life would end. She was killing me slowly, projecting all of her suffering and anger unto me. And I felt them, akin to jagged blades at my skin, which despite the fact that they were invisible, felt all too real.

There was a weak ruffling all of a sudden, which was followed by Emily's barely audible plea. "Stop... Stop! Don't hurt him!"

"You will stay quiet!" Alexandra ordered. "This does not concern you. None of this would have happened if it wasn't for you. If you had kept yourself hidden, he would be mine completely."

The next thing I heard was Emily choking, clearly at Alexandra's mercy.

"Yes, well you stole her body. I think that involves her!" I defended, trying for distraction, but clearly failing.

"Wyatt, you may need to reevaluate your loyalties, darling," she said as if she were scolding a child, and that only fueled my anger.

"I should be loyal to you, is that it? Unwittingly follow a being that has done nothing but lie to me? A being that has no issues with taking possession of another's body? I will not!"

"Wyatt, stop..." Emily called to me, interrupting my tirade.

She had taken us back into our safe space. "You took us out of there pretty quickly this time," I huffed, trying to catch my breath after the sudden shift.

"Thanks. I think I might be getting the hang on how Alexandra would steal you away. Not that I would ever do that to you."

"I know," I soothed, sensing her agitation. "How did you do that?" I asked, curiously.

"I think I just had to calm myself down enough to concentrate on getting us out, and then we were here. I don't know how long it'll last, so don't get too confident. Listen, her fight is not really with you," she clarified, and I tried my hardest to calm us both.

"So you say, Emily. But she is adamant about hurting you, and I cannot let that happen! I need to keep you safe. I love you."

"I love you too, Wyatt. We have to do something, because we can't just stay here as puppets for her to manipulate."

"I agree."

"Let's take care of her together," she said, her tone suddenly filled with strength and determination.

"Alright, we will," I agreed, hoping that it would work.

Chapter 12

We wandered aimlessly for what seemed like days, trying our best to come up with a plan that would set us free, as well as get rid of Alexandra somehow. "So we're back here again," Emily sighed, reclaiming my attention, "with no plan whatsoever."

"So it seems," I agreed, feeling utterly useless.

"What are we going to do, Wyatt? We can't keep living like this," she said, and in her tone I could hear despair, as well as the dark tones of defeat.

When a tinge of frustration began to well inside of me, I faced her, and she went silent almost instantly as the air filled with a staggering heaviness. The desperate expression on her face alone was enough to disarm me.

"I know what to do," she sighed, her voice filled with resolve.

"Emily?" I called, fearing this sudden change around us. What had she decided?

"I-I can't tell you," she whispered, and the strain in her voice made the air around us seem heavier somehow. Saddened.

"Why not?" I asked, becoming increasingly more agitated as fear clawed its way into my heart.

"I just can't, Wyatt. You'll just have to trust me. Can you please do that for me? It will be safer this way. I promise. Please?" Again, her tone spoke of something that her words seemed to keep hidden, something that I was not likely to agree with, but I could not force her to tell me what that was. I was afraid of where her thoughts might lead, but there was nothing that I could do about it. I would just have to wait and see what happened.

"Alright," I sighed as a way to appease her, but I could not help feeling uneasy still. *For now*, I thought to myself.

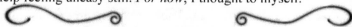

We spent a month in peace, the passage of time made obvious from the outside by the rising and setting of the sun in the horizon as it emblazoned the pages with gold. Over our time together, my feelings for Emily grew exponentially, and this surprised me because they felt completely different to those I had harbored for Alexandra.

I could now see that those had been forced and stagnant, almost as if they were not my own. Whereas my feelings for Emily felt alive and thriving. Naturally, I was worried about her. Especially as I felt that there was something wrong. She was keeping something from me, but I had no idea what that could that be. Despite how much I tried to persuade her, she would not tell me anything. In fact, she only seemed to retreat further into herself as time went on. I had no idea of what was wrong nor of what I could do to help her. The only positive aspect in this situation was that we had little to no encounters with Alexandra, which was a welcome reprieve. The encounters we did have she would appear as boastful and cunning as usual, but would leave us quickly. This was a welcome change that at the same time filled me with dread. *What could she be planning?*

The sole evidence of her continued presence was the faint winds that carried an eerie hum with them, a sound that seemed to vibrate throughout the pages. It caused a bit of trepidation in me, and I had to come to terms with the fact that it would drive me mad.

Adding to that madness was the fact that Emily seemed to be growing weaker. She had never truly been happy here, and I could not fault her for that when I considered our circumstances, but recently it felt as if she was giving up completely. "I cannot lose you Emily. I..." I cut off as desperation stole my voice.

"You won't," she assured me in a breath. "I promise."

"How can you promise me that when you get weaker with every passing minute?" I asked.

"I..." she stalled, and I could not help interrupting.

"You cannot. So please stop telling you are 'alright'," I emphasized, "because we both know that you are not. Something is happening to you, Emily. Now, what is it?" I asked, my voice lowering to a dangerous calm, and I felt her crumbling from within before I heard her speak a word.

"I-I don't know." Her voice sounded hollow and pain ridden, a ghost of her usual lilt.

"Emily, please, tell me what is wrong?" I knew that I was nearly begging by this point.

"Y-you can feel this?" she asked, shivering as sadness crept into her voice, a murmur that was becoming increasingly hoarse. "I don't w-want you to feel this pain."

"Well, I can. Clearly not as strongly as you, but... Please, tell me what is wrong."

"I don't know what's wrong! I feel so strange. Weak... In pain... There's so much pain..." Her voice quickened and slowed until it finally ended on a broken whisper, cracking from her inner chaos. Her situation, her pain, had consumed me to a point where my afflictions seemed to fall to the wayside of my mind. My sole focus was on helping her. My life be damned.

What happened to me no longer mattered, because I knew that I would gladly take on all of her pain if it meant that she would not have to bear it. The suddenness of this situation also added to my state of unrest, because she had seemed perfectly safe and healthy just moments ago, but now it appeared as if she were being torn apart from the inside. As my distraction dissipated, I found that my own insides soon mirrored hers. The pain was excruciating, but I knew that I could not dwell on it. I knew that I had to focus on her.

"Emily, can you hear me?" I asked, my teeth grinding as Alexandra's torture persisted, seeming to escalate as time went on.

"*Mmm,*" she whimpered, the sounds of her shallow breathing reverberating all around me, and they made me fear that I might be losing her.

"Emily, listen to me. I do not know what is happening, but you need to hold on. Do you hear me? I will not lose you," I emphasized. "Do not force me to live without you! I love you!"

"And I lo-ove you. What is this, Wyatt? What's going on?" she asked, her voice frantic as she tried to inhale around the pain.

The strength of her affliction nearly sent me reeling. "I don't know, dove," I answered, feeling helpless. What was wrong with her? It seemed that had turned into my perpetual concern. I could sense only a faint echo of what she was feeling. By her tone, I knew that it had to be so much worse. "Emily, dear one, we need to understand what is wrong with you. I'm scared for you," I said, my voice catching.

"I'm scared too," she replied, her voice trembling, but she appeared to calm almost instantly.

"What is it? What is wrong?" I asked, anxious over another possible fit of suffocation at the hands of our tormentor. "*Alexandra!*" I shouted, unaware of the moment.

The air around us stilled and grew with the heaviness that I now knew so well. I wanted nothing more in that moment than to rip her to shreds for everything she had done to Emily, to us, but I knew there would be no way for me to do that. "*Yet,*" I seethed.

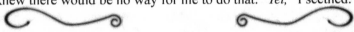

Even though she tried her best to hide it, I knew Emily continued to suffer, sharp echoes of her pain becoming a part of me as well. We were linked after all. And now we were both at the mercy of Alexandra, making me hate her all the more for it. I knew that the only way to truly free us both from this was by killing her, but I couldn't think of a way to do that without Emily finding out and trying to stop me somehow. And what if I failed? What if she tried to hurt Emily again? I couldn't withstand that. But I have to do something.

Chapter 13

In the early morning, Emily was woken by yet another bout with pain. Alexandra had never really released her from the throes, only lessened their intensity, and then increased them when she wanted. The pain rendered Emily completely exhausted, and though she tried to hide it, her labored breathing betrayed her.

I wanted nothing more than to end Alexandra's life. What was stopping me? Simple. I knew that Emily was likely to follow me, or worse, try to stop me by any means necessary. That would surely lead to disaster, and I was not about to put her life in danger. I had to think of a way to end Alexandra in secret.

"G-good luck w-with that," Emily said, her breathing short.

"Emily, you know it has to be done." I sighed.

"N-not a-alone," she gasped.

"You cannot come with me. She would kill you, Em, you know that!"

"But sh—"

"She won't kill me. She may hurt me, but she won't kill me. She 'loves' me, remember?"

"That's not love," she scoffed. "Alexandra's o-obsessed with you. If we ever get o-out of here, remind me to s-show you some movies on the subject, o-okay?"

"Alright," I agreed, thankful for this comical exchange which served as a distraction to our problems for the time being. I was also happy that she could see a life outside of our prison. She had not given up completely on the possibility of getting out of here. Without knowing, she had provided the perfect means for me to distract her. I proceeded to ask her all about movies, which ones were her favorites, which ones she did not like, and which ones she would watch with me. I was still worried about her though, because I knew that she was still in pain regardless of her trying to deny it. I wanted to call her bluff, but I knew that would only agitate her even more, so I decided against it.

"How do you know so much about this time? I thought that Alexandra trapped you here years ago," I trod lightly, unsure of how she would react to my question.

Her sudden change in mood proved me right. "I guess I was given some free rein, or maybe she just wasn't as attentive to me since she had her hands full with you. So I was able to keep track of the outside world, even though I wasn't a part of it."

"Wyaatt..." a voice called out in a whisper.

It was sickeningly sweet, and I felt a chill run through me as soon as I heard it. The feeling was all too familiar, and I knew exactly what it meant. "Alexandra," I called out, shock and annoyance lacing my tone.

"Wyatt..." she called again, her voice soft, yet menacing somehow. The voice then changed to that of the girl I loved, leaving me confused.

"Emily? Em! Are you alright?"

"Wyatt? I'm okay. I'm right here, shh..." she comforted, and I realized then that my voice was nearing mania again.

"What happened to you?" I asked, my emotions chaotic.

"I don't know!" she cried, her voice rising with fear and frustration. "It's... it's like I'm not myself anymore, Wyatt. I'm so scared."

"I know you are, but I'm here for you, alright? I won't leave you. I promise," I vowed. I felt my emotions radiate outward, coursing through my limbs, so strongly that I thought she might actually feel them through my touch.

Her wide eyes and surprised demeanor confirmed my suspicion. "How are you doing that?" she asked, wonder breaking through the tension of the moment.

"I don't know, but I'm damn well glad that I can," I said, as I felt our skin react to each other's, becoming substantial with every touch.

"Wyatt look..." Emily gasped, looking downward.

"I know," I said, as I saw my skin as well, a rich copper illuminated with a mysterious inner glow. Hers was a beautiful creamy color, just visible within our transparency. "May I..." I trailed off, my nerves becoming palpable as I felt a light hum inside me. The air around us suddenly filled with nervousness, heavy and all consuming. "Don't be nervous, Em," I soothed as the question arose again inside my mind.

Her reply drifted in a gentle gust that caressed us both.

"I'll take that as a yes," I laughed as I reached out to her. As I took her into my arms I felt her warmth, as I always had even before I was able to touch her. Our skin reacted to one another's, and everything seemed to be rushing by me, but also there was an eerie stillness at the same time. As we were emoting, the world around us responded accordingly. I didn't know what was happening, but I could feel that something was coming. Something was going to happen, and all I could do was wait for it.

Chapter 14

"What do you think that is?" Emily whispered, and I felt her as she rested her head on my shoulder. She felt warm and electric, which radiated throughout my body as I held her.

I felt something cold and dark seep through me suddenly, and it robbed me of breath as it ran through my chest. "Do we really need to ask? Alexandra is still around, and I can feel her getting stronger. That scares me."

"I know she is..." Emily said, her voice drifting off with sadness, almost as if she was giving up.

My fears grew exponentially at her tone. "Hey, hey..." I soothed, sensing she needed it. "I'm the one that freaks out, and you're supposed to kick my butt when I get like that. Remember?"

She laughed softly. "I know. I know. I'm just tired of all of this," she sighed, her voice wistful. "I just want to go home."

My heart ached for her, and my anger at our situation only increased, which surprised me because I did not think that I could hate Alexandra any more. "Listen to me," I told her, my voice solemn in spite of my anger. "I will get you out of here. Do you understand me? Somehow, we—" I stopped midsentence, getting a sinking feeling that I was not going to be with her when she left.

"Wyatt?" she called, no doubt noticing the change in my demeanor.

"It is nothing. Do not worry. All we need to focus on is how we are going to do this."

"Right," she said.

A wall appeared out of nowhere, suddenly blocking my connection to her. I could not sense Emily at all, and was afraid that it was due to more of Alexandra's antics. "Emily!" I called.

"I'm here, it's okay..." she soothed.

"What was that...?"

"I've been practicing with..."

As she trailed off fear made its way through me, because I knew what she was doing then. "Emily, you can't. It's not safe for you to do this!"

"I can do this, Wyatt. I've been working with it for a while now."

"What?" I cried out in panic.

"It started after she kidnapped me. It was like she absorbed me somehow, and then spit me back out," she explained, and I felt her shudder. "I fainted afterward, but when I woke up, I felt this energy inside me. It seemed very faded though. Just a hum. That's why I could barely talk to you in the beginning. But it's getting louder. I don't know why, or how, but it is. I can feel it," she explained, her voice a mix of wonder and fear.

"We will figure this out, Emily. I promise you that."

"Would you like to see what I can do?" she asked, swiftly changing the subject. Her tone shifted to reserved excitement.

I agreed with the sole purpose of giving her a means of distraction, but in reality, I was afraid of what she might be capable of. It was obvious that there was a change in her. As hard as I tried, and regardless of her trying to play it off, I could not ignore it. "Emily..." I trailed off.

"I'm fi—"

"Do not. Say. You're. Fine." My teeth grinded, and my voice was clipped with rising anger. "Because we both know that you're not."

"Well, then don't try to play the hero! I can save myself."

"I'm not saying the opposite. I know you can, Emily. But I want to help you, because I love you." I felt her start to calm down. Her anger lessened with every breath she took. I knew that her emotions took a lot out of her because she always felt them so strongly. I'd do anything to spare her all of this, but I had yet to figure out how to do that. "I'm sorry, Emily. I didn't mean to—"

"Forget it," she sniffed. "We're both stressed out, and I'm not feeling the best at the moment."

"What do you mean?" I asked, trying for casual concern. I was able to take in even more changes in her. How her voice's timbre would change as she spoke, and the heaviness that accompanied her, which had everything to do with her sadness. It was as if a weight bore down on her. All of which scared me to death. I contemplated telling her, but was afraid of the consequences, of her reaction to what I thought might be happening, and it scared me so much... Because if I were honest with myself and with her, I would have to admit that I thought that she was being overtaken by something. And since we had yet to hear from her, my worst fear was that the one taking over Emily was Alexandra. I did not know how I knew, just that I did. I was losing Emily, and that scared me out of my mind.

No, I thought to myself. *I will not lose her. I will not let that happen.*

"I'm tired, Wyatt," she sighed. "I'm going to sleep okay?"

"Yes, and I will watch over you," I told her, coming out of my mind. I felt her smile, a tiny ray of light coming through a cloud gathering.

"That's just slightly creepy, you know," she quipped.

"Rest now, Emily," I whispered. "I love you."

"I... I love you too," she replied.

I felt the instant she fell asleep, and as I listened to her breathing, I was glad that it sounded relatively calm. Emily needed more calm in her life, but I knew that would not happen while Alexandra watched our every move. And Emily could not stay here forever.

No matter how much you want her to stay with you. I scoffed at my thoughts, annoyed at them for popping up unbidden, and also stunned at how selfish they made me feel. And I did feel selfish, because I wanted her with me, regardless if I ever had the chance of getting rid of Alexandra or not. Did I really expect Emily to stay in this prison with me, if she had the opportunity, however slim it might be, to leave this place one day? Would I be so selfish as to keep her from a life that she was entitled to live? Would I dare keep her from finding someone other than me to love? The last question that came to mind seemed to weigh my heart down heavily in my chest... I certainly hoped that I would not.

Chapter 15

Alexandra

"Where could they be?!" I cried out in frustration, because both my love and the nobody had gone missing and I had yet to find them. I couldn't even feel them anymore. Regardless of my anger, however, I found Wyatt's growth absolutely amazing. He was now taking initiative, being strong and caring... Loving, even!

Albeit, toward the wrong girl. The specter, the weakling I took this body from, I thought, stroking my arm. I was becoming consumed with thoughts of him someday touching me, loving me with the same fervor as he appeared to love the wench. I did intend to get him a body as well. He would have to earn it, of course. He would have to show me that he would be unwaveringly faithful to me, which he had failed to do so far.

I should have turned the girl when I took her body, as I had with all the others, but I had needed to keep her in the beginning to be able to anchor myself to the body, and as time wore on, I became careless in not disposing of her. I was aware of the same link between us as I was of the link between myself and Wyatt, but in my hubris, I chose to disregard it.

But since discovering that I could use that to aid in my finding them, they seemed to have begun to block me, rendering the connection useless. Could they have learned of the link as well? But how could they know of it without...

No, that couldn't be. They could not have been using this... this weakness on my part against me, could they? The mere thought of this filled me with a rage and hatred toward them for intending to take my chance at happiness away. That same anger and hatred burned me for letting them get away with that. I wanted to see them both suffer for it.

I loved Wyatt fiercely, but if he wouldn't mine, he would be no one else's. He had seemed to be my one successful creation out of countless others. The bookstore was filled with my past attempts, which I kept as reminders that I visited to keep their memory alive in my mind. They could still be felt, most of them in the faintest of ways, mere whispers of their former selves. I had loved them, created them just as I had created Wyatt to be mine, yet they had been laden with imperfection.

89

Wyatt also had his weaknesses, clearly, having gravitated toward another. This was a betrayal that I could not take lightly, and I could see myself hating Wyatt as much as I loved him. I supposed that I should blame myself for leaving them alone for so long, and not sensing that the wretch was siphoning my powers. I would have to admit that it took me a while longer than it should have to realize what was happening, but slowly, I began to feel the transfer.

What made me increasingly furious was the fact that I had made myself vulnerable to this from the beginning. I had gained a body, but she would, in turn, gain my powers. I would not stand for that.

That damned link. I should have been aware of it sooner. And the wretch had been growing irritatingly stronger, stealing my powers. And now she had conjured a barrier between us.

She made me so angry. I wanted her dead. And yet, I knew that if I had killed her too soon, I would run the risk of this damned link killing me as well. I felt anger and frustration roil inside me like a coiled snake waiting to spring unto its prey, my nerves quivered from the tension. I would have to make sense of all of this and find a way for it to work in my favor.

Chapter 16

Wyatt

I watched over Emily as she slept, her soft breathing was a welcome reprieve from her turmoil. My love for her grew with each passing day, and her confidence appeared to increase as she revealed more of her heart to me. I knew that her stubbornness stemmed from fear, but I was thankful that she allowed me to experience more of her lovely soul as time wore on. I alternately loved and hated everything she revealed about herself, the dark aspects from her past as well as positive attributes of her family; and I bore a special kind of hatred toward the abuse she suffered at their hands. So in some ways I felt good about her being here with me. I knew that was an insane viewpoint, but I would prefer we stay here under Alexandra's thumb while unified, than to have Emily go back to a situation where she was most definitely unsafe but alone.

Contradictory but I knew that we could hide from our captor indefinitely if need be. Even though that was no way to live a peaceful life, when I thought of her returning to her world...

As those thoughts began to wander away, I began to focus solely on Emily instead, as a wave of dread came over me. A halo appeared around her, black and faded, undulating as if it were a living thing. I reached out to touch it, feeling dread and sick fascination as it began to wrap itself around my fingers in a loving manner, very different from how it was handling Emily. Desperation rose within me, and I tried to coax the shadow away from her. It seemed to be caught between pleasing me and staying with Emily, the danger becoming obvious from her pained expression.

"Shh," I soothed. "You need to let her go." I had expected it to ignore me, but was amazed when I noticed it hesitate before returning to her. "Hey, hey look at me," I said nervously, trying again to get it to leave Emily alone.

With a whimper and sigh, the being finally released her and came over to me, enveloping me in warmth. It seemed perfectly harmless around me, but I knew better than to believe it had been that way around Emily. It weaved around me softly. As it came in contact with me again it stung, which almost made me cry out in pain, but seemed to dissipate and become a soft hum around me.

"What are you?" I asked, my voice a mixture of curiosity and fear.

The reply came by way of a giggle that was by no means pleasant, but it offered nothing else.

"Aw, did I scare you? I'm sorry," I apologized, and its energy shifted again to outright flirtation. What the hell?

The giggle then intensified to a laughter that chilled me to my core, fading as quickly as it had come. I expected it to ignore me, but was amazed when I noticed it hesitating before it went back to her.

A giggle and sigh came from nowhere, sounding distinctly like that of our foe.

"Alexandra!" I growled, tired of her charade. A thought occurred to me in that instant, and I returned to where Emily had been. I knew that I had nothing to lose after all. "Alexandra!" I called out again, this time in a more soothing, coaxing manner, but no answer came. I was not foolish enough to expect one, honestly, even if I kept trying. That would have been too favorable to me, to my sanity, and I had come to know her as someone who did not care about that. My anxiety escalated and turned to anger with each of my cries. "Alexandra," I called, my voice strained. "Answer me! Please..."

Her amorphous laughter sounded again, and suddenly Emily began to stir, and I ran over quickly to where she lay. Her form seemed to flicker in and out of existence, taking my nerves with it as each breath became shallower.

"Emily, sweetheart, stay with me. Please," I whispered, begging her.

"Wyatt, it's her," she cried out, her voice strained. "She's been around me for a while now, doing who knows what. I think she's trying to get rid of me."

"Do not strain yourself, please. Just breathe for me. Like this," I said and began breathing in rhythm. Slow, even breaths, which she proceeded to replicate with her own. We had created our own little bubble within this sanctuary; one that I hoped would help Emily heal.

"I think—" she began.

"Don't," I interrupted, admittedly more forcefully than I had meant to. "Forgive me, I... Do not say it, please. You. Will. Be. Fine. Do you hear me?"

"*Yes,*" she conceded, albeit reluctantly.

I knew that was not the truth, and yet, I had no proof to give her that would verify my statement.

"What?" she asked, trying to guess at my thoughts from my reaction.

"I just wish that I could make it easier for you to believe me." I sighed, grappling with the emotions that were surging inside of me. "I want nothing more than to see you safe."

"Nothing more? Really?" she asked, a smirk evident in her tone, and I could not help laughing from amazement at how her mood would shift so quickly and affect mine in kind. Her happiness, though tenuous, found its way to me quickly.

"I will not let her take this away from us, do you hear me?" I said, fervently.

"I believe you," she whispered, and I felt her gaze on me. "I love you."

"I love you, too."

All of a sudden, there was a searing pain in my chest which nearly knocked me out. Alexandra always resorted to wounding me. Did she have some obsession for Shakespeare or something? I knew that Alexandra was attacking us both when I felt Emily begin to crumble beside me, our connection making it possible for us to share the pain. I tried to siphon as much of Emily's pain to myself in order to lessen her pain from this ordeal, but she would not let me. She was handling our joint affliction, and reveling in the fact that she could.

My admiration toward her increased tenfold, strengthening my affection for her which in turn seemed to fan Alexandra's ire. I thought I might have gone crazy when I began to enjoy it. Not only was I reveling in my love for Emily, but as I fought for it, I felt my strength growing, and I liked it.

"Wyatt," I heard Emily call to me. "Be careful. She's trying to feed off of you."

"I know, I promise I will not let her. I love you."

"I know you do," she replied, her blush palpable through our connection.

"I doubt that. But alright," I teased, trying to lighten the moment a bit.

"Hey..." she replied, feigning hurt.

I reached out for her, a joyful laughter bubbling from inside of me at the fact that I had been given the small miracle of touching her, of being able to feel her as I held her. My nerve endings reacted as if lightning coursed through me at the slight contact.

"That feels... Do you feel that?" I whispered, wonder housed in my tone. Amazement had pretty much taken up residence in my mind, and undoubtedly hers as well, and refused to leave.

"What is that?" she wondered, sighing at the feeling.

"I have no idea, but if it allows me to feel closer to you, then I count it as a positive," I said, honestly. She sighed happily in response, and I felt a light brush upon my hair, a whisper of a feeling really, but there nonetheless. "I am glad that still works," I joked, but really, I felt relieved that I still was able to sense her.

"Me too," she said earnestly. "I couldn't go back to not being able to feel you."

"I understand what you mean, but..."

"But what?" she asked, clearly uncomfortable, and I thought that my being forthcoming with my feelings again was for the best.

"I am afraid, terrified really. Sometimes I don't know why, but others..." I paused and shook my head to clear it. "Sometimes I feel as if I'm about to lose you."

"I feel like that too sometimes, like I'll just keep losing myself, fading more and more every day until there's nothing left," she said, her voice trembling, "but then I hear you and it's like you keep me tethered to you. You make me feel safe. Protected. And that helps me not feel so scared anymore."

Her words warmed my heart, the evidence of this spreading around us and charging the atmosphere around us.

"That feels good," she commented, her voice clearer, stronger almost.

"Are you doing that?" I asked, awe clear in my tone.

"I... I think so," she stammered, obviously stunned.

"How?" I breathed.

"I don't really know, but I've been hearing her in my head," Emily replied, and anger surged within me at the mention of Alexandra. I wondered when, if ever, we would be free of her.

Chapter 17

Emily

After we'd finished talking, I told Wyatt that I was tired and needed to rest for a while. I hadn't been lying really, because I really did feel exhausted, but that wasn't the only reason I'd needed time to myself. The truth of the matter was that I was no longer just focusing on my misfortune, which if I was honest, I'd brought onto myself.

I had always focused on how my life would have turned out if I hadn't stepped inside the bookstore. If Alexandra hadn't trapped me in here for the past.... How many years had I been in here? My heart ached when I thought of how much time I'd wasted in here, and how if I hadn't abandoned my friends that day to wander off, I would have been with my family.

No, scratch that. I would have coped with my family situation for only so long, but I liked to think that at some point I would have had the courage to look for a way out. Though it certainly wouldn't have been this. I blamed myself for having wandered into a place that clearly wasn't open. I blamed myself even more for getting sucked into this mess, but when anger started to come to the forefront of my thoughts, I chose not to focus on it.

I chose to focus on Wyatt instead. He was the only reason I stayed relatively sane throughout this time, being able to focus on someone other than myself and the fact that he needed me. That hadn't been the only thing occupying my mind though. There was also the not so positive fact that I had been feeling less like myself with each day that went by. I could feel myself slipping away more and more, and it was scaring the crap out of me. The only solace I'd been able to find had been the reprieve from Alexandra, regardless of not knowing how it happened or how long it would last.

Where had she disappeared to? I knew that I was tempting fate by thinking about her, that I was practically calling her with my thoughts, but I couldn't help it. I didn't believe that she had disappeared forever. Not at all. Because that would have been too easy.

It would mean that Alexandra had given up, but if I knew anything from the years that spent trapped by her, it was that she did not give up. Nor did she offer the slightest bit of mercy unless she could gain something from it. She was extremely manipulative, to an extent I hadn't thought anyone capable of.

She had supplanted me flawlessly. In the beginning I was so mad when I watched her take over, thinking that my friends and family should have been able to tell the difference between me and Alexandra, but as time passed I began to notice just how she had mastered everything in my life, right down to most minimal of details. My mannerisms, my speech patterns, everything. In the end she had replaced me with no one being the wiser. I couldn't find it in my heart to hold anyone accountable, when even I could see how alike she made us seem in the end. The fact that she had replaced me so easily in the eyes of my family, of my friends, made me bitter. I mean... they were supposed to know me better than anyone, right? I had almost lost all hope, had almost become apathetic and shut myself off because I was hurt and betrayed, and almost became consumed by those feelings.

As the sadness that these thoughts caused me started to take over, thoughts of Wyatt seemed to break through it, like sunlight breaking through gray clouds. Thoughts that led to others that only made me angry, but for an entirely different reason. How twisted could Alexandra be to inflict so much unto someone so innocent?

When I watched her create Wyatt, I knew she would become territorial and overprotective. But she took those emotions and elevated them to an obsession. It took months for me to be able to contact him, and even then I knew I was risking backlash. I didn't know why it hurt me when I saw how much he trusted her, when I saw how he believed that she was innocent of anything and everything.

It helped me to focus on things other than the ones happening to me, like the fact that I could interact with Wyatt and tease him for his growing feelings for Alexandra... ew. He hadn't liked that, but it was ridiculous to me. I mean, he'd hardly known her and he'd "fallen in love" with her. What was that about?

I mean, I knew about insta-love in books, and it had always rubbed me the wrong way, but to actually see it? It looked like brainwashing to me. How could anyone want to lose themselves like that? I mean... How would things possibly work if you didn't know anything about the person you had those feelings for? It aggravated me to no end, seeing him follow her around like a little puppy. He was a classic Yes-Man, and it was pathetic. I'd made fun of him, but in reality I'd been frustrated and fighting back the urge to smack him in the back of the head.

Had I been jealous? Maybe. I hadn't known I was going to fall for him, and I still didn't know how that had happened to be honest. What I did know was that I was already in deep, and I didn't want to get out of it.

We had become each other's safe havens, but more than that, he became someone I could care for, and maybe even love without having to be scared of any double edged sword. I couldn't think about that right now, not when we were both in so much danger. I didn't believe for one second that we'd seen the last of Alexandra, not when I still felt tethered to an invisible weight that crushed me whenever it saw fit. I also refused to believe that if she were truly gone, I'd remain stuck here.

Life could not be that unfair. Knowing her though, that was exactly what was bound to happen. I was never getting out of here....

The only positives I could see in this situation were that I had Wyatt by my side, and that I'd never see my father again. I'd never have to deal with his abuse or his manipulations again. He'd never lay a hand on me again... Positives. Stick to the positives.

Chapter 18

Wyatt

When Emily went to rest, I could not help worrying about her. She had seemed fairly well before, but I could feel a gradual shift in her. I knew that something had been weighing on her, a darkness that grew with each passing day, which brought my fears to the forefront of my mind.

What if Alexandra was not truly gone? I had not voiced my fears because I didn't want to frighten Emily, but I couldn't help thinking about it. This was not the first time either, but I could not ignore it anymore. Not now that the changes in Emily were so blatantly obvious.

Her demeanor had become more subdued, as if the energy that had drawn me to her had all but disappeared. It tore at my heart to see her like this and not know what to do. It was Alexandra's fault. It had to be. This thought chilled me so deeply that it felt as if my entire body was frozen. I knew then that Alexandra would not rest until I became hers in body and soul.

And even though the thought of giving myself over to Alexandra in any way seemed worse than any torture she could conceive of, I would do it, if it meant that Emily would be spared. If it meant that she could have the life that she deserved, even if that life did not include me. I would forfeit my happiness if it meant that she would be safe. I shook my head, hoping to free myself from all those thoughts that haunted me. I knew that I needed to focus if Emily and I had any chance of getting away.

"Alexandra, I know it's you. I know you're still here somehow."

The answering laughter, so deceptively innocent, shook me further and seemed to cleave me in half. She was alive, and surely biding her time until she again wreaked havoc on our lives. My hands clenched into fists at the thought. If that were the case, I wouldn't hesitate to wring Alexandra's neck, and I would count each breath as they left her body until there were none left. A shudder came out of nowhere, light but obviously present around me.

"Emily?" I ventured, still able to feel her presence, regardless of how light it was. "My love, are you there?"

As a response, I heard breathing, light and distant but continuous, which made my heart burst from happiness and relief.

"Emily..." I called out, my desperation nearly tangible. Her lack of answer nearly drove me insane. I had heard her, felt her even, so I knew in my heart that she was alive, and that I would do whatever it took to get her back. As for Alexandra, I wouldn't rest until she suffered for what she had done, for the lives she had destroyed. My heart filled with rage. Fear swept through me then, so overwhelming, so crippling, that it rooted me in place. Fear for Emily, fear for myself, and fear for what Alexandra's actions were creating within me. This seething hatred that was once foreign to me, but now seemed natural. Innate.

Emily

Moments with Wyatt almost made this hell I'd been living worthwhile. I'd watched over him ever since he was created, not in any creepy stalker way. Ever since that day though, I'd felt a pull toward him, like something that called me to him for some reason that I still couldn't figure out. I'd read about things like this in books all the time, but I never thought it was really possible.

Then again, how could I call anything that I'd been through, what Wyatt had been through, possible? This would only be believable if you read it in a book, something straight out of the YA section.

Maybe I can write about all this if we ever get out... Yeah, right. Like that will happen. Who would read it anyway? My thoughts started to wander when I felt the surge. It had been happening a lot recently, leaving me drained. Sometimes it just lasted moments, while other times, it took me days to recover. A monsoon that seemed determined to follow me wherever I went; and I seemed to absorb the downpour, to take into myself everything it gave.

At first I was terrified that this was just another ploy of Alexandra's, one that would finally get me out of the way for good. But lately, I'd noticed that the winded feeling I'd get seemed to give way to stronger inhales, the energy around me seemed to soak into me. I could feel electrical currents raging through my blood, my phantom skin prickling.

It scared the crap out of me. I knew it scared Wyatt too, especially since I kept most of this to myself, and also because I disappeared so much. Even though he'd tried to downplay it, his concern was like a living being that made itself known the moment his bravery took center stage. And even though dauntlessness was appreciated, it was his concern, hidden beneath which comforted me the most and kept me grounded.

"Well, isn't that sweet?" said a deceptively kind voice that sounded and felt too familiar, a voice that sent a sense of foreboding straight to my heart.

"No— it can't be," I gasped, my mind rebelling against the sound of her voice, already screaming at me to run, but she just kept me rooted in place.

"But it is. Why do you want to run off so quickly? I just wanted to talk to you. You see, it seems that you have two instances of thievery against you."

"What are you talking about?" I asked, even though I had a pretty good idea of what she was talking about.

"Do you mean to tell me that you haven't felt any differently? At all?" She asked, almost innocently, her gaze shifting from the concern of a mother, to the predatory glare of a snake. Sicko. "It seems that by some twist of irony, my powers spread to you when I trapped you here..."

"And it's been like a magnet ever since," I interjected as things finally started to make sense.

"Precisely," she sneered. "A sick twist but one that will soon be remedied."

"W-What does that mean?"

"Haven't you felt it? The waning in your energy, a tug of war, if you will. That is simply the power that you stole, trying to return to me," she finished with a deadly whisper.

And there it was, the explanation to everything I'd been feeling. Now fear sprang forward as I began to think of what she might do to retrieve them. I knew that the target on my back had just become that much more valuable.

My breath came out of me in a burst when I suddenly felt Wyatt's warmth around me, like a cocoon that would shield me from whatever harm I'd face. But I was tired of being the fragile flower.

"You idiot. What are you doing here?" I scolded half-heartedly.

"I knew that you needed me, so instead of trying to break through her walls and likely getting caught, I tried sneaking around yours," he explained, and I could hear the playful smirk in his voice, as well as the instant that it turned to hurt. "Why did you hide all of this from me?"

Shame rippled through me because I'd known I could trust him, that this concerned him too, and I'd still kept things to myself.

"Because I'm a stubborn idiot," I confessed shamefully.

"Yes, you are," he allowed, mockingly. "But I still love you."

I smiled, knowing he'd forgiven me, and I sent my love to him through our connection. "I love you too," I added for good measure, as I dared myself to feel some semblance of happiness in this moment. Challenge accepted.

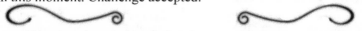

Waves of rage crashed through our little bubble then, one after the other, all coming from Alexandra's direction. They seemed to get stronger every time they hit, and I could have bowled over from the pain, until Wyatt created a shield around us.

"Maybe I inherited some powers as well," he said with a knowing smirk as he helped me. "I would like to try something," he suggested. "Would you put your hands on mine?"

I responded by giving him an unsure look, but agreed, and hissed from pain as the air hit the gashes on my skin. As our hands floated over me, I started to feel tingles along my injuries as they started to heal. I could feel the cuts knitting together, and leaving faint white lacelike patterns on my skin. "What the hell?!" I cried out in shock as I looked them over, tracing them lazily with my fingers, all the while feeling a mix of horror and curiosity. I looked to Wyatt, and my eyes almost felt wild as my fear grew. I had no idea what I was dealing with, much less how to handle it, and my breathing started to escalate, its rhythm going off kilter as I felt myself falling down a familiar rabbit hole…

"You took my powers from me, Emily, and I think it's time that you returned them."

I started to heave as I felt my throat constrict and my lungs felt as if they'd been lit on fire. Her favorite punishment. "And just how am I supposed to do that?" I asked, feeling the telltale shift around me then. Her— my powers making their presence known.

That's when it clicked. They had been her powers, but from the moment they'd touched me, I could and apparently did make them mine. I didn't have to fear them, because from the moment they'd manifested in me, in Wyatt even, they had been ours to wield. The fear I'd felt for so long had started to fade, began to give way to resolve, and a strength that I never thought myself capable of. I now knew that Wyatt and I could escape, that we could vanquish our demons together.

"It would be wise for you to figure that out, my love," she said, and I was again thankful that I could feel myself fighting her intrusion into my mind. One of the rare perks of having been trapped for so long was having the time to learn to defend yourself.

When Wyatt called me back, he brought me out of my head, and got me away from Alexandra, allowing me to focus on something other than our tormentor.

"What does she want?" Wyatt asked, his voice grave.

"She wants her powers back," I sighed. I was surprised to note that my voice didn't sound fearful, but annoyed. These powers had become mine. They were such a part of me now that I didn't think there was a way for her to get them back.

Chapter 19

Alexandra

I was biding my time at this point, waiting for an opportunity to be able to take back what was mine. And even though Wyatt was being difficult, I knew that would only be temporary. That it would only last until we were both on the same terms. Until she was no longer a part of his world, and I would be able to take her place. Permanently.

It had been so easy to replace her the first time. No one had been the wiser. Her family, her friends had all embraced me, and accepted me as her. I had even felt pity toward her when I found out how her family treated her— me— but I had remedied that a long while ago, and even had the courtesy of telling her that her abusers were no more.

That I had killed them after her pig of a father dared to lay his hands on me. And his new love had just stood there watching in shock as I rendered him. She then had the nerve to wield a knife at me! I knew that she wouldn't surrender, really, and thought that the determination that coursed through her would have made us good partners.

But it was not meant to be. Even after freeing her of all that, the whelp had still betrayed me, had still poisoned my love against me. I knew that I might have to end him as well and start anew, create another not so easily swayed, but to do that, I needed my powers back.

Wyatt

Emily was nearly frantic when she found me. She said that she had seen Alexandra, had heard her speaking in her mind. What she heard had obviously shaken her deeply. She explained that it had not been the words that had been spoken, but the memories and the thoughts they had brought on. She had also confessed, rather sheepishly, that after talking about the specifics behind her parents' deaths she could feel some relief from that part of her life. She also explained the grudging gratitude that she felt toward Alexandra in that respect, but that hearing those words had brought all of those feelings back. Feelings that she would rather forget.

"Is that stupid?" she asked.

"I do not think it is. They may have been your parents, but they turned your life into a nightmare. I think that it is perfectly normal, as well as expected, for you to feel relief when that part of your life is not there anymore."

As I said that, I could feel her heart crack open, and the dam that held her tears back broke apart. She began to cry silently. As those tears quickly gave way to sobs, I could feel her tears soaking into me. I would absorb her pain and gladly make it my own if that eased her suffering.

"Let it out, my dove," I whispered soothingly, listening to her broken breathing as she clutched at my chest in clear desperation as she tried to hold on to anything that might keep her grounded. "I will be your anchor if you allow me to be, just as you are mine," I whispered to her, and I kissed the top of her head.

She nodded. "I love you. So much," she breathed.

I quickly decided to hold onto her in that moment as my mind called forth images of pillars, each one strong in their own right, joining together to make an even stronger structure.

"What's with the towers? Don't turn all Colin the Constructor on me now," she teased.

Her breathing sounded clearer, and her calmer demeanor let me know that she was feeling better, but... "Who is Colin the Constructor?" I asked, curious.

At that she burst into laughter, and tears were again evident in her voice, but not the kind that I was worried about, because I could feel the lack of pain in them, which was enough for me. For now.

After some prodding on my part, she began to tell me about her childhood, keeping strictly to the happy moments. One of which was the children's TV show, she'd explained.

"I was a bit old for it, but it kept me from focusing on what was happening, you know? It distracted me. The theme song was pretty catchy too," she said, and then proceeded to hum the tune.

I smiled and hoped that I had helped her put aside the thoughts that plagued her, that I had helped ease her suffering, if only for a little while. "Can I ask you a question?" I began quietly, knowing that I would be treading dangerous waters.

"What?" she asked warily.

"How did it happen? How did she trap you here? Tell me what really happened. No sugarcoating, please," I expelled in one breath.

"That's actually two questions. And two statements," she replied, trying to be comical and lighten the mood, no doubt, until I gave her a look of incredulity. At which she giggled half-heartedly and sighed. "I'd been fighting with my parents; dad liked to get handsy, and mom wouldn't do anything to stop him," she began, her voice only seeming to deaden as she continued. "Sometimes I felt like she turned a blind eye on purpose. Anyway I try to look at it, it always seems the same. My mom just didn't care about me enough to stop him." She had stopped at this point. It was obvious how much it affected her.

"Emily, it's okay. You don't have to tell me anymore," I told her as calmly as I could, considering what she had just revealed. The thought of killing the man was not far from my mind.

She shook her head. "I need to do this, more for my sake than yours."

I knew she was right, that she needed to get this venom out of her system, so I told her to keep going, and promised to keep my threats to a minimum. That made her laugh.

"The day I went to the bookshop was one of the few days that I had to myself. My friends jumped at the opportunity," she said, smiling fondly. "They'd figured things out pretty early on, and started coaching me, telling me that I should go to the police."

I nodded in full agreement with her friends, and she smiled.

"Anyway, at some point in the day, I'd wanted to go to the bookstore while they'd wanted to do something else... I don't really remember what it was. So we separated, agreeing to meet back up at our favorite dessert shop. You know why I never made it back." She flew through the rest, assuring me that I had been aware and present for it. I knew of nothing better to do than to stay quiet. I couldn't believe everything she'd gone through, couldn't believe she was still alive after all of it.

"You are strong," I stated honestly, to which she snorted.

"How am I strong? I've been a coward, hiding since this whole mess started."

"You keep on living. Day to day. That is your strength, that despite everything, neither Alexandra nor your father could keep you beaten down." Her answering smile felt genuinely thankful, no pretense of strength as in other instances, and I was grateful because she was showing me her true self.

Chapter 20

Emily

I'd finally decided that these powers belonged to me. No matter how they'd been used before, or by whom, I was now going to use them for good. I was still scared of facing Alexandra. I didn't feel ready to confront her at all, but I knew it had to be done at some point if I wanted at least one shot at getting Wyatt and myself out of this mess.

He'd volunteered to help, serving as my target, and even though I'd been against it many times, he said he saw no other way, and I had to agree. I knew I had to get in tune with these abilities, had to at least practice so that there would be no surprises in the future. However long that might be for me.

I closed my eyes and took a deep breath as I tried to get a feel for the energy that coursed through me. At first, everything was silent, blurred, my view clouded. No evidence at all of the powers that I'd gotten from my tormentor. As I focused though, honed in on the energy, it seemed to manifest itself in the shape of a big lynx, fierce and beautiful. I stood there frozen, because it just kept staring at me as if it couldn't look away. I couldn't either.

"Are you mine?" It seemed to ask, the question somehow as clear in its eyes as its voice in my head was.

"No," my voice shook from nerves. "I think you might belong to Alexandra."

He instantly recoiled at her name, and the hiss that came after was one that could make the bravest of hearts tremble.

"What can I do?" My voice dripped with helplessness, but I instantly felt an inexplicable tether between us, one that seemed to be growing stronger the longer we stared at each other. I had no idea how to handle this, because I didn't know the first thing about magic, let alone if I wanted to deal with it.

"I can sense my essence within you. You only need to embrace it and I will follow."

"What about Wyatt?" I checked. "Would he be unprotected? I mean… You belong to him too don't you?"

"His power is his own. He was created, and so Alexandra had to give of herself, of her magic to him."

"So Alexandra…" I dragged on, severely confused.

"She is hoarding whatever vestige of power she still possesses. That is why I appear to you in this form, because I am not whole," it explained, gesturing to itself with its paw.

"Would you still look like this?" I asked before I could stop myself, and at that moment I knew I had made my choice. And he knew it too. I could feel his jovial laughter inside my chest.

"I would take whatever form you choose, mistress."

"Keep this form, it's cute," I smiled. "But don't call me mistress, okay? I won't own you."

We laughed as we looked at each other, and I felt a further cementing of the bond between us. I felt like I was welcoming an old friend home.

When the lynx joined me, it seemed to welcome everything that I had to give. The power within me was helping it grow stronger somehow, and I swear that I could see it growing in front of me. Gone was its unstable appearance, its body having grown more powerful from our link, which I could feel radiating from my own. The most beautiful part of him by far was his eyes. Where they had been wary and sad before, they glowed with strength and love now… For me?

"Yes, for you. You've already proven yourself a kind and gentle wielder, and my appreciation for that knows no bounds," he replied with a light head-butt to my hand.

When he lingered under my hand, I gave into my curiosity, and began to pet him. He licked my hand and I couldn't help laughing.

"What happens now?" I asked, weaving circles on its head playfully.

"Now we wait for her to find us," he replied simply, obviously enjoying my attentions.

"And then what?" I asked nervously, but somehow I knew what he would say before he said anything.

"Then you will take what belongs to you," he replied with a wink and a playful growl. "You should return to him now. You will need each other more than you know."

I agreed and gave him a hug around his neck, promising to return as soon as I could. He, in turn, promised to strengthen and watch over me always. I got ready to leave and find Wyatt, but couldn't help crying a little, because I was leaving something that had become very important to me. No matter how short our acquaintance was. He gave me another head-butt, and this one told me to move toward where I needed to be, so I left to join Wyatt and clue him in on my plans.

Wyatt

My anxiety grew as time wore on. I had no idea what was happening, or how long Emily would be gone. I just knew that I stood by and watched as she had drifted away, disappearing from in front of my eyes. The emotions I felt were not solely mine, and were confusing as they shifted from fear to trust, from uncertainty to a fierce determination.

Was she in trouble? I wanted nothing more in this moment than to follow after her, to protect her from whatever she was facing, never stopping until she was safe. All the while, I reminded myself that this had been her choice, and I would not take that from her, knowing that she could handle this and more. Believing that she could.

So I resigned myself to watch over the place where she had been as she took on whatever obstacles she was dealing with and hoped that she returned to me soon. I wished that there was a way to help her, to calm her tempestuousness, but knew that I could not. This filled me with an instant peace, letting me know that she could manage whatever she was facing.

All I could do at this point was stare impatiently at the place where she had just been, looking for any sign of her. Her emotions, which were not very comforting at the moment, were all that I had to guide me. So I resigned myself to watch a blank space as she faced whatever obstacles she was clearly dealing with, as helplessness overpowered me throughout the entire ordeal. Ironically, it was her silence that affected me the most; I had become so accustomed to the gentleness of her voice that not hearing it now was jarring, and added to my worries. After all, I knew of Emily's strength, trusted in it in fact, but I could not account for Alexandra's. She was just that unpredictable, unrecognizable to me, despite the fact that she was my creator.

Something had to be done, but I did not know what that was, and the realization filled me with despair. So I decided to close myself off to that feeling, and just focus on my connection with Emily. As a result of how consumed I was in my thoughts, I had neglected to focus on her and had lost it. When she returned to me what felt like days later, I had confused her presence with Alexandra's, and prepared to defend myself accordingly.

Had I not felt Emily's essence come over me, I feared that I would have followed through with it, damning everything we had worked towards. Her mere presence was soothing to me, and I wished—not for the first time—that I could take her in my arms, and never her let go. I had to make sure that she was alright first. As soon as I decided to reach out for her, she opened her eyes to meet mine. I could see the smile that she reserved just for me. I was so thankful for her in this moment, and for having her with me, that I had nearly forgotten about her disappearing. But not entirely.

"Are you alright? What happened? Did she hurt you?" I panicked, having come to the worst conclusions where she and Alexandra were concerned.

"Shhh," Emily soothed. "I'm here, I'm alright. Nothing bad happened to me."

I felt an overwhelming need to verify this, but I trusted her to tell me the truth, so I accepted it for now, but I was not willing to give up on this subject forever. "Alright, so what happened then? I could feel something happening to you, and it scared me to death!" I called out, making her flinch.

"I'm sorry… I got so wrapped up that I forgot about our link. Things got really intense there for a while."

"I know. Please tell me what happened," I nearly begged as I searched for any sign of wounds on her. Thankfully, I found none, and the next words to come from her mouth only confused me.

"Oh, Wyatt... It was great!" she exclaimed, tears evident in her voice.

"Come again..." I said, snapping out of my thoughts, which were now laced with incredulity. In that moment, I felt the need to search her mind for signs of lunacy. Thankfully, I found none.

"I was looking for something to help these powers make sense, and boy did I find it! No... that's not right. It found me!" Her excitement radiated off of her, making her glow from within.

I smiled in spite of my worries, because her happiness was just that infectious. "What happened to you?" I asked, needing to know.

She replied by becoming incredibly still and breathing deeply, and I watched as the glow appeared to increase, becoming almost blinding. A hum made its way into my ears, and then seeped through me, seeming to amplify something similar from within.

"What was that?" I asked, my voice raw from shock, as she then began to explain about Alexandra's powers, and how they appeared to be manifesting in her. All of this information swam inside of my brain, and I felt myself reeling. "Emily, wait," I interrupted when none of it seemed to make sense to me. "So we both have powers... and a... pet?"

"You could say that," she agreed, laughing. "Though he's more mine than yours, but I can share."

"Well, that is good, I guess," I said, trying to lighten the mood further. "I would not know how to take care of it." We both laughed then, feeling lighter than we had in a long time. We were not alone anymore, and from what Emily had explained, it seemed as if we never were. As if *I* never was... But even with that knowledge, I would never want to miss out on meeting her, because I couldn't see my life without her.

Chapter 21

Emily

"So, how did this happen?" Wyatt asked after I'd told him my secret. Our secret.

"I don't know," I confessed, never having really stopped to think about it. "But I think we might have a fighting chance against her now, you know?"

"We might, but how do we know that she has not caught on yet?"

"It's just a guess. While I was with m—" I stopped, shocked by how nice it felt to claim the lynx as mine. "Nothing happened while I was with my lynx." Pride and gratitude were obvious in my tone, and was immediately serenaded by a purring in my mind. I laughed as it tickled my ear, and I also laughed at Wyatt's cute confused expression. "It's Lynx," I explained, trying to calm down my excitement. "He's very playful. With me anyway."

Wyatt smiled, but I could tell that he was suspicious about all of this.

"What's wrong?" The question slipped from my lips before I could catch it. His expression was making me nervous.

"It's nothing. I just have difficulty trusting something that could potentially betray us."

I flinched at the accusation, and dove right into the lynx's defense. "He's not hers, not anymore, I promise. He'd never betray me."

"Should I resent it?" he joked, and I nodded, giggling.

"Oh, you definitely should," I joked back. "He's much cuter."

Wyatt and I were laughing together this time. I felt the lynx's approval as he joined us, and like a cat curling up to his owner, he cozied up to me. My mood, which had been all over the place, started to settle down with his presence. That's when I knew that I had another anchor on my side to keep me grounded.

"You change when he is near, have you not noticed?" he asked, getting out of my head.

"What do you mean?"

"You seem happier, as if you forget about all of this for a while. I think that might be your escape."

"I didn't think about that…." A blush made its way to my cheeks, and I felt the light brush of his touch on my face.

"I love that about you," he commented happily.

"It's not very nice when people can tell what you're thinking just from looking at you," I grumbled. I tried to change the subject as subtly as possible, but I think he knew, which only annoyed me. "Would you like to see him?"

"Could I? You would not mind?"

Obviously, curiosity had won out… good. "Of course not. I'll go find him. Wait for me, okay?"

Wyatt agreed and I set off to find my friend.

I knew that I needed to be alone to reach the connection, for now at least, so I'd asked Wyatt to leave me alone for this.

He agreed only to appease me, but I could tell that he hated the idea of leaving me, because I could feel his restlessness. Nevertheless, I convinced him that I had to do this alone, and promised him that I'd be careful. I calmed myself as much as I could, tried to remember if there was any way that I could make him come to me.

"You only have to call on me," Lynx responded suddenly, and laughed at me.

I knew I would've jumped if I could have. "You scared me!" I told him in mock reprimand.

"I know," he replied mockingly, and we laughed together. I was amazed at how fast our bond had been formed and at the strength it already had. "Because I actually want to bond with you," he said, giving me a gentle nudge. "I never wanted to bond with Alexandra, and she mistreated me because of it. She wanted to change me to fit her whims."

As he spoke, his anger and fear came over me, making me shudder. "Is sensing each other's feelings part of our link?" I asked as I tried to comfort him.

"So it would seem. This is as new to me as it is to you, after all. I have never experienced it," he thought out loud, and my mind couldn't help echoing the sadness in his voice. I wasn't sure if I should call attention to it, but I broke down and reached out to him, emanating the love he was missing and clearly needed.

"It's alright. You don't belong to her anymore. You don't have to belong to me either if you don't want to." Pain speared me when I said this, because of the closeness I already felt to him. Even though the thought of losing him hurt, I knew that I would let him go if it made him happy.

"Silly, I love you. I will always be yours," he purred.

Wyatt

I watched on, feeling helpless, as she fell into the usual state that she always did when she interacted with the lynx. This used to scare me to death, but I had learned to handle that fear, since I knew that I could never convince her to stop, no matter how unsure I was about all of it. I did not trust it when Emily had first told me its origin, and I still didn't. How could she ask me to put any faith into something that might very well be Alexandra in disguise? This was, after all, the source of her powers. As the thought came to me, I began to fear for Emily, for her overly trusting nature, as well as her growing power. Temptation came to me as I thought of all of this.

I wanted to trick this being into leaving her alone, if not to kill it, so that we could find our way out of this place, to keep any vestige of Alexandra away from Emily. The need for this coursed through me, livening up my phantom limbs, to the point where I could almost believe them to be real. It strengthened me, and I reveled in that feeling, which both scared and propelled me forward.

A change was coming over me, one which became more evident with each passing moment. A change that I had no control over. The only thing that I knew deep within my bones, was that I would never be the same again.

Alexandra

Damn Wyatt, and damn the specter. I had seen no sign of them in months. Regardless of my searching, there had been no advance in finding them. They were clearly good at hiding, but I needed to find them quickly, because I could feel myself growing weaker with each passing moment.

My powers were being stolen from me. I had gone from being annoyed with their antics, to feeling downright livid when they disappeared. Especially with Wyatt.

How dare he leave me when I had given him so much? How dare he throw all that I had given to him in my face? My anger had been aimed at only one perpetrator during all this time, and I was trying to rationalize another's role in my mind, but I had to accept the fact that there were two perpetrators now, the thief and her follower. Wyatt had betrayed *me*, the one who had given him life, and he had chosen to love the one who had become my enemy.

Chapter 22

Emily

Leaving the lynx's side hurt me, as in actually affected me more than I thought possible. The pain started almost immediately after I'd left him, and felt like an amplified separation anxiety, which only seemed to get worse as time went on. The fact that I was starting to get used to it was both a relief and saddening to me. I knew then that I had gained an ally, a friend for a lifetime, but I had no idea how long that would be.

I remembered trying my best to keep away from him, fighting my curiosity from the day that Alexandra had created him. The curiosity drew me in, but fear kept me away. The fear that he might turn out to be like his creator. I'd been wrong though, clearly, and now I was ashamed that I'd ever compared them. But how could I make peace with Alexandra trapping me here, and her creating the man I fell in love with?

"You should not, because she created me for herself, and never counted on my falling in love with anyone but her," Wyatt whispered in my mind, and I almost screamed.

"Don't do that!" I whisper-yelled, wanting to punch him right then. "I hate it when people sneak up on me..."

"I'm sorry," he laughed, but got all serious suddenly. "I really am." His presence seemed to be getting stronger somehow, like he was becoming tangible, but that was impossible. Right? "I don't know... I feel it too, but I do not want to get my hopes up," he responded to my thoughts again.

"You know that gets a bit annoying sometimes, right?" I mocked, laughter clearly in my tone.

"You love it," he replied boldly.

"What else can I do?" I sighed, pretending to be annoyed. The truth of the matter was that no matter how much I tried to fight or ignore it, I knew that I was in love with Wyatt. It had built up so slowly that it happened without me noticing. The second that I did, I was already in too deep. And scared out of my mind from it too. But all I could do at this point was ride it out, and pray that the consequences weren't something that I would regret later.

Wyatt

Grappling with feelings that had previously been foreign to me was getting easier with every passing second. They fueled my resolve to end Alexandra's existence in order to gain Emily's and my freedom. Even though I had begun to factor in the effect that this could have on my life as I knew it, I also knew that I would sacrifice myself if it meant that I could gain her escape from here.

"Wyatt?" she called, awakening from another fainting spell. "I do not faint!" she cried out defensively.

"You should not read my mind if you will not like my jokes..." I defended myself, laughing.

She huffed prettily, shifting to her beautiful laughter almost instantly. Her recently mercurial, erratic moods fascinated me. How she could be so upset one minute and happy the next, I did not know, but I chose to put it aside to study later because enjoying her happiness was my immediate focus.

"It's every girl's dream to be able to read her boyfriend's—" She stopped in the middle of her remark, and blushed instantly.

I could not help but laugh. Her blunders were my happiness, because they were further evidence of what we shared. "I believe that is the first time I have heard you call me that," I teased. The truth of the matter was that her statement, though brought on impetuously, caused me so much joy.

"Well, t-that's what you are, i-isn't it?" she asked, stumbling over the words, suddenly timid.

I laughed as a reaction to my own nerves. "Yes, I am. And I am glad you will have me."

She searched within me in that moment, and found that I was so happy, that I was on the verge of doing cartwheels. That fact, in turn, made her more exuberant, more comfortable with expressing her feelings. I could, however, sense the ever-present fear acting as a deterrent, but I knew that she would not want to discuss it.

"You are such a dork." She laughed.

"But you love that about me, do you not?" I defended.

"True... so we're official now?" she whispered, and the insecurity in her voice stung a bit, but I knew we would be able to work through this somehow.

"I guess," I acquiesced, intending to diffuse the intensity of the moment, so as to make it more comfortable for her.

"I... didn't want to assume," she mumbled shyly.

"Assume away."

The air around us charged in that moment, with an energy that seemed to seep into me, giving me incomparable strength; a strength that I had not felt until that moment. It was amazing, but frightening at the same time.

"Emily..." Her name left my lips in a whisper as the energy flowed through me, seeming to undulate as it made contact.

"I know," she acknowledged, happiness evident in her tone, "that's him. He's a part of you too, you know."

"Who?" I asked, distracted, my mind consumed with what I was feeling.

"Lynx, of course," she explained, giddiness overtaking her. "He's letting you know that he's yours too. Took him long enough."

I could not help but notice her tone change from comforting to slightly annoyed, but I was too transfixed to respond. I felt as if I was meeting someone for the first time, but also as if I had known this being my entire life. As if they had always been there, watching over me.

The thought filled me with anger, but brought tears of joy to my eyes as well, because I had never truly been alone. Even before I had discovered Emily's existence, someone had always been there. The realization that I was not alone, that I had never been, even before discovering Emily's existence, was almost too much for me to handle. On the one hand, there had always been someone watching over me. While on the other, this being had sat idle as I had meandered, lost in my own thoughts and fears. Never once caring if I had needed guidance... or comfort.

"I'll leave you two to talk," Emily told me quietly, and I grimaced.

I was thankful that she seemed too preoccupied to notice, but I also felt hurt for that same reason. I could feel myself becoming unstable, on the edge of madness from everything that was happening, and I didn't know what to do. I was afraid to tell Emily, afraid to admit my weakness to us both.

Confusion encompassed my mind immediately after she left me to talk to this being. What was I supposed to say to it? What could it possibly have to say to me?

"That remains to be seen, does it not?" A voice seemed to chuckle in my mind.

"I thought that you two would be talking..." I trailed, having nothing better to say.

"Emily and I have already made our peace with each other, and now it is our turn," the lynx said, suddenly appearing in front of me, and nudging me with its head.

I did not understand why, but the casual manner in which it had spoken her name sparked anger within me. How could this being, which had only recently made itself known, be so quick to form a bond with Emily? How could it pretend to hope for a bond with me? Just the thought of this filled me with anger, which I made no effort to keep hidden.

"How could I not have heard you until now? Where do you get the nerve to show yourself *now*, after all this time?" I asked.

"You really are her creation," it mused with a laugh.

"What is that supposed to mean?" My voice nearly broke from anger. Having had no previous contact with this being, it was nothing but a mere stranger to me. I only knew of its existence because of Emily, and yet, I could not help feeling the connection it professed.

"Chaotic, selfish, deceitful. You think only of yourself," he answered calmly, even though it felt as if he had shouted the words at me. "You think that your worries are aimed at Emily, but truly, it is only you whom you consider. You have not expressed your fears to her, even though they pertain to her as well."

This statement brought me up short as guilt began to eat away at me. I had asked Emily to trust me with what was happening with her, but had not offered her insight into my state of mind in return. It was fear that kept us both from being honest with one another.

Emily

"Wyatt, what's wrong?" The question burst from my lips as soon as I had detected the change in his emotions after the lynx had left. I could see the same terrifying signs that I'd seen in myself for a while now. That fact chilled me to the bone. We were both being overtaken by something dark, both succumbing to our fates in this in-between, surrendering to Alexandra. His choice looked like it had already been made.

"She won," I breathed, finally voicing my biggest fear, and I could feel my heart breaking at the thought of it. "She got to you, didn't she?"

"Maybe. I don't know... What are we supposed to do?" His voice sounded defeated, while also sounding laced with hatred. I knew that this was killing him, that it was turning him into someone I wouldn't recognize, and it scared me. Reaching out impulsively, I wanted to soothe him, to do anything that might help him, but I couldn't, because he'd put up a wall in his mind that kept me from communicating with him.

"Let me in. Please..." I almost begged.

"I cannot..." He trailed off, his voice breaking as it drifted off. "I have been... feeling strange, and I am afraid that I might hurt you."

"What? Don't be ridiculous. You would never hurt me," I defended him.

"Emily, I have not been completely honest with you. Something is wrong with me. I feel as if I am losing myself."

Hearing the painful tremble in his voice hurt me. It made me realize that both of us were on the same dangerous path. Neither of us could do a damn thing to help ourselves, much less to help the other. I could hear the shame in his voice too.

To me it seemed like we were both losing ourselves, and neither of us knew how to help ourselves, much less how to help the other. No matter how much we wanted to. That's when I decided to bite the bullet and express my thoughts.

"I've felt it too... And I think I know what it is…." I trailed off, afraid that actually talking about what was happening to me would make it seem more real, but Wyatt was able to tell anyway. He had already sensed the inevitable in me. In both of us. "There has to be something we can do." I wasn't willing to give up. I'd started to before he came into my life, and I'd been miserable. Now I wanted to fight. For my freedom. For his life. For our revenge.

Chapter 23

Alexandra

The silence had become nearly maddening. Where there used to be several voices in my mind, a way to keep track of my quarry, their presences seemed to have vanished. My concerns shifted, however, as I had begun to feel my powers draining slowly from me. A process that had been happening for a long time, and had clearly gone on undetected by me. I knew the reason behind it now, though. That stupid lynx had likely severed its connection to me, thereby cutting off my connection to my strength, and as a result, had also affected my powers. I had not felt any pain, because ours had never been a true bond born from love, being instead forged from my needs and desires. Yet I owned him, just as I owned Wyatt, regardless of them having been stolen from me. My plan was beginning to take shape, had already been set in motion. Its effects were slowly taking hold, the transference becoming more evident with each passing moment. It would not be long before the whelp's body became fully mine, and she would cease to be a concern.

Wyatt was another story, however. I feared that all of my hard work with him will have been for nothing, and had to decide if I wanted to begin anew or help him forget his dalliances, all the while ignoring the pang of disappointment from possibly losing such a promising prospect. I could remember the moment when I had created him, could remember the blind trust that emanated from him. That Wyatt was no more, however, after having become contaminated by the specter planting the seed of doubt in his mind in regards to me. I had tried to bring him to the truth, to the realization that no matter how hard he tried, he would not survive without me. Nevertheless, my efforts were proven null, and regardless of my endeavors, I was unable to procure his heart. He had clearly fallen prey to her web of lies, had ceased to be mine from their first interactions, which I had been too preoccupied and careless to prevent. I had begun to remedy this however, and could feel the results of those efforts, a process that had taken time, as well as so much of my energy, but which I knew would be worthwhile in the end. I knew that the process had been halted though, as I could no longer feel the flux of energy. My anger heightened as I realized the cost of my stupidity. I had unknowingly given them a key to their escape. Thoughts of Wyatt had consumed my mind, and in doing so, had effectively cloaked my eyes to what was happening. But that blindness was only temporary, the damage they had wrought was minimal, if not reversible. They thought that they could keep me in the dark, ignorant to their plans, and that they would succeed in escaping from me. Not if I can help it. I have sacrificed too much to forfeit now. They would pay, and Wyatt would be mine.

Wyatt

I shuddered as something made its way through me, a feeling so real, so dark, and foreboding that I could not help fearing for Emily's life, as well as my own.

"That is her," the lynx offered as it appeared from out of nowhere in my mind.

"What do you mean?" I asked, my voice sounding forced as I tried to remain civil.

"Alexandra has begun to lose control of everything as Emily has been absorbing her power. What we are feeling is nothing more than Alexandra's retaliation," it said languidly.

"Can't you do something?" I yelled, my anger and frustration finally spilling over.

"I am afraid that I cannot, for I am merely a carrier, a vessel for my master's powers."

"I knew that you couldn't be trusted!" Anger and betrayal took hold of me. I thought of our potentially fatal mistake in following this being, not to mention the speck of faith I had placed on it.

His laughter sounded in my head, almost condescending. "Why must you be so quick to judge? You did not even infer as to whom I was referring to."

My anger seemed to dissipate at his statement, giving way to a quiet surprise. "Tell me, then," I demanded.

"My master is Emily," he revealed, leaving me speechless.

I couldn't fathom how this had happened. Did she know?

"Yes, she does," he assured in thought.

"Stop that..." I berated.

"How?"

He spoke to me of his origins then, of his time under Alexandra's control, and of how Emily had set him free and how he had ultimately chosen her as his.

I listened, amazed and proud of Emily, and then began to think of all the repercussions this would affect.

"Our Emily is truly one of a kind. She has all the strength and abilities needed to confront Alexandra. All that is missing is belief in herself."

"She always has been. It's baffling how she can't see it," I mused aloud, and saw the lynx give a thoughtful shrug as he stared into my eyes. "You really do care about her, don't you?"

He nodded, and gave me a playful head butt. "I care for both of you. You are just stubborn. Too stubborn to see that maybe?"

Anger, shock, and embarrassment battled inside me at his comment. I wanted nothing in that moment other than to lash out at this self-assured know-it-all. "You really have some nerve, don't you?" I seethed. "How dare you think that you know anything about me? You may have been present throughout my life, but you never made yourself known, so guess what... That makes your point null and void."

Lynx waited patiently, timing his breathing, almost as if coaxing me to follow his beats. "You need to release your anger if we are to work together, Wyatt. If not for you or for me, then please think of Emily."

Her name brought me up short and seemed to halt the storm that I felt within me. "I always do," I whispered, chagrined. But truthfully, my prejudice had inundated my thoughts when it came to him. My apology came through gritted teeth, reluctant and resigned. I would do anything for her.

"Would you let her go?" he asked calmly.

I could not help but feel panic set in immediately. "Why would you ask me that?" The question shook in my throat. "I can't answer that question!"

"You need to prepare yourself for any and all possible outcomes," he reasoned.

"I don't know if I can, but if it's for her benefit, I would like to think that I would try my best."

The cat nodded, seeming to find my answer satisfactory. "You will be good for each other," he commented casually, and I felt as if I had finally gained his blessing.

A validation of sorts. My breath left my lungs as the tension eased. I did not know how much I had needed his approval until I had received it, and now that it had been given, it was time for me to focus on other matters.

Emily

I was so wrapped up in my thoughts, that I completely missed it when lynx came up to me in silence. When I finally did notice him, it felt like my breath lodged in my throat. I would have jumped if I could've. "Hey," I whispered, trying to downplay the knot in my throat. "Where have you been?"

"I spent some quality time with your beau," he answered, and I blushed at the title, my feelings radiating around me.

"How did it go?" My voice shook with nerves that I had no explanation for. I knew that they would need to hash things out at some point, but I thought that would happen later on. I was grateful though, because maybe now I wouldn't feel like I had to choose sides, or have to talk to them separately. Both of them had become my family after all.

"He told me of his grievances, and I quelled his fears. It went as well as could be expected."

"That's not a comforting choice of words, you know..."

"Do not worry, Emily. All is well between us. I promise you."

"He's right," Wyatt said, appearing from out of nowhere.

I felt his calming presence take over immediately, starting to soothe the roughness that my worrying had caused me.

"Hey," I sighed, relieved. "How are you?"

"I'm alright, I promise. Now my only concern is you."

I could feel myself blushing, the reaction making itself known as I made the temperature around us rise unintentionally, but I didn't care because I was happy. Both beings I cared about were with me, and I could feel our combined strengths flow between the three of us. Not only did I feel that strength combo, but I also felt a love so fierce, that it almost overwhelmed me. Lynx and Wyatt were the only ones that made this bearable, and I didn't know what would have happened to me if it wasn't for them. Tears came to my eyes the more I thought about it.

"Why are you crying, Emily?" Wyatt asked soothingly, and I felt his light touch on my cheek.

"I just love you both so much," I answered sincerely, yearning to hold them both in my arms for real. I could feel my thoughts veering toward another dark place when Lynx jumped in.

"We love you too, Emily. Forever."

Ours was a bond that would not be broken easily, and I knew that we would protect each other, no matter what we had to face.

"I'm glad that all is settled between us, but we shouldn't think that this is the end of our problems. We still have to deal with Alexandra," Wyatt said, jarring both me and Lynx back to the present.

"Way to dampen the mood, Wyatt," Lynx and I grumbled playfully, and I tried to downplay the sudden surge of nerves that came over me too.

"I have a feeling that we're in for something big, but somehow I know that we'll be okay," he commented, giving me hope.

I nodded. "Well, good." The strangeness I'd been feeling pretty regularly now was rearing its ugly head again, and it was stressing me out. "Lynx, I'm scared," I admitted through my link with him, because I didn't want Wyatt to worry.

"You know what is happening, Emily, and you can't keep it from him much longer. He needs to know," Lynx told me, confirming my suspicions, and I nodded woodenly.

"She's trying to take over... What can I do?" My voice shook with desperation.

He looked at me then, and something in his eyes calmed me down instantly. "You and Wyatt each have a piece of her within you. Use them against her."

Past thoughts came flooding back into my mind from out of nowhere; thoughts of my waning energy, and also of the surges of power that I'd felt from time to time, which were now stronger and more frequent. Could that really be Alexandra's powers? Did Wyatt feel like this?

Lynx's comments made me concerned that Wyatt had also been going through this, and I felt guilty about keeping it to myself. Maybe if I hadn't, we could have figured things out quicker, and beating myself up over this wasn't going to fix anything. I knew that. So I decided to put those thoughts away to look at later. What was important now, was learning to handle what was happening, and how to fix it. In all the years I'd been here, I hadn't been very proactive in regards to my escape, and I knew that was all on me. I had to start getting more proactive if I wanted to get out of here. I felt the power—my power—running through me, and the realization that all of us, Wyatt, Lynx, Alexandra and I were connected dawned on me. Would we ever get away from her?

"I may be a connection, but I belong to you and Wyatt. You freed me," he soothed through our link.

"Not really," I regretted. "You're still connected to her, and she could still tap into that connection."

"You must give me more credence than that, Emily," he mocked, but then turned serious. "I vowed to protect you."

"I'm sorry. It's just that she has so many ways to attack us, and—" My voice shook as I spoke.

"And you still fear becoming like her," he spoke, his tone questioning and confirming all at once.

I agreed, knowing it was pointless not to, and that he would be able to see through the defenses I had put up. "I do, but I know you are right," I breathed, knowing that I had to get that fear out of my head somehow. I just did not know how.

"You will never fully be rid of it, Emily, but you must overcome it if you want yours and Wyatt's freedom," he spoke after reading me.

"How?" My voice sounded pleading, and I realized that I'd come to need his guidance.

"You have to sacrifice yourself."

"W-what do you mean?" I asked, my voice so thin that it cracked.

"You know what I mean. We have thought about it plenty of times. Certainly you have," he commented seriously, and that's when I knew that I would have to take over to beat Alexandra at her own game.

"Wyatt can't know," my voice shook. "I want to protect him. To keep him safe from her as I possibly can."

"He is bound to have figured it out on his own, Emily," Lynx reasoned. "He is just as smart as you are, after all."

"That's exactly why I've kept my thoughts to myself. I've been blocking him to keep him out of danger," I admitted quietly, feeling ashamed that I'd been hiding all of this from him, but if any of us was going to survive this, some secrets would have to be stay secret.

"He must know, Emily. We all need to be prepared," Lynx advised in a tone as if he knew what would happen in the near future.

"What do you know?" I whispered, my voice shaking from fear and exhaustion.

"Only that Alexandra will use any means necessary to reach her objective."

The truth of the matter was that I didn't need any reminders, because I could feel it happening, and had to fight it off constantly. Exhaustion was the most frequent parting gift left over from the endless tug of war I was dangerously close to losing.

"Enjoy the time you have left," whispered a voice that seemed to come from deep inside me, sounding equally threatening and comforting.

"Alexandra..." I called as my voice trembled.

"Shhh, I promise this will be quick. Utterly painful, but quick," she smiled, and I started to scream at the top of my lungs when I started to feel like I was being torn apart.

Wyatt

I jolted awake with a pain so acute that it was almost maddening, a pain that I recognized immediately as Alexandra's calling card.

"You are right, and Emily went to her," the lynx explained, his voice simultaneously grave and resigned.

I felt something drop within me when I thought of Emily being anywhere near her, and that only fueled my anger. "And you let her go alone? Just like that? What happened to looking after her?" I raged.

"She is not alone. Remember that I am just as much a part of her as I am of you, so I am with her even as I am here with you," he replied, and my tension released instantly at his words.

Although I couldn't help feeling as if there was more that I could do to aid Emily.

"You will, in due time," the lynx answered, easing me.

"When all of this is over, we need to set some bounds. You really should stay out of my head."

His reply was accompanied by a shrug and some purring.

"What happens now?" I asked, fearing the worst.

"All that is left is the hope that Alexandra underestimates us all," he said calmly.

"You sound eerily calm about all of this..."

"What is that phrase... 'Fake it until you make it', isn't it?"

I nodded in response, laughing shortly because I recognized the phrase. He laughed along with me, and that was when I realized that, along with Emily, Lynx also made all of this mess bearable. And in that moment, I also realized that I didn't know what would have become of me, if it wasn't for the *both* of them.

Chapter 24

Alexandra

The push and pull had become a thing of normalcy. A tug of war between Emily and myself. And she was proving a more formidable opponent than I thought she would. Who would have thought that the meek flower would grow thorns? Thorns which seemed to be poisoning my happiness. All I wanted after all, was to live my life with the man of my creation, but her possessive streak came to the forefront as she took hold of Wyatt and the carrier, refused to let them go. Refused to let them be mine.

Now I was forced to fight them all, to be able to keep that which belonged to me. My love and my powers. I would have to replace them and begin anew of course, hopefully with a better outcome. Replacing the carrier would prove more difficult however, as magic was free willed when young, and took centuries to tame. I had obviously been unsuccessful.

Again.

The anger that resulted as I thought this over took hold completely; a blinding, consuming rage that radiated inward as well as out. My incompetence served as kindling. As the fire within me ran its course, I resolved that rather than beginning anew, as I had countless times before, I would regain what was mine through any means necessary.

The pieces were already in place, all that was needed was for things to run their course. There was a level of uncertainty however, a resistance which unsettled me, further demonstrating my lack of control for the situations at hand, and my inability to secure my goals. I did see a glimmer of hope however, which was enough to keep those objectives clear.

Emily

The pain was excruciating and familiar, but I was thankful that this wasn't my first experience with it. Because of my previous bouts with it, I was better at handling every onslaught that came my way. That didn't mean it sucked any less though, and I couldn't say the same for my fears, which obviously still affected me. You can't have everything though, right? Guilt stopped my thoughts.

If I hadn't gotten trapped in here, I never would have met Wyatt or Lynx, and I couldn't imagine my life without them in it now. The love between Wyatt and I had grown so much that we couldn't see a life without each other, which was amazing and terrifying all at once. I had also started to think of our lives outside of this mess, which was dangerous in and of itself because it gave me hope. I mean, would I have a life outside of this place? Would he or Lynx?

"Don't think of that now," Wyatt soothed, reading my mind again.

I smirked, my blush making itself known from the telltale warmth that surrounded us.

"I think that it has a mind of its own," he joked, making me giggle.

"You may be right," I agreed, shoving him playfully. "And. Stop. Reading. My. Mind."

He laughed with every shove, and he kept on teasing me. We were behaving like one of those super sweet couples, and just thinking about that scared me to death.

He became serious very quickly. "Why are you afraid of this? Of us?"

His questions jolted me as if it had physically electrocuted me, and I felt horrible. "You know why," defeat coated my words, made them each as heavy as bricks so that each one was difficult to get out.

"No, I don't, and I would like to."

He sounded angry, hurt, and I couldn't blame him for it. "Because I don't want to hurt you!" I yelled, the frustration bubbling inside me and cracking my voice. I knew I was unstable, the constant shift between Alexandra and me becoming more obvious with each day that went by. This had become a game of cat and mouse, and she was a relentless chaser.

"Emily..." Wyatt called, his voice breathless and shaking. "Why didn't you tell me?"

Well, I guess the cat's out of the bag now. "Because I wanted to keep you safe," I admitted. "I thought that if I kept it to myself, it wouldn't affect you."

"That's not how this works, and you know it!" he cried out, clearly angry.

"I was desperate, okay?!" I yelled, airing my frustration. "But it was pointless, obviously. She's going to win no matter what. Whatever we try won't matter. Nothing will make a difference." I sounded pathetic, and I knew it. The years of torture finally weighing on me, making me feel utterly defeated. Dealing with this for as long as I have, had taken a toll on my psyche, my emotions, everything.

The tension was tangible in that moment, I could feel it as if it were a breathing creature at my neck, but I was tired of this game, and I'd be damned if I let Alexandra control my life anymore. "Emily, please reconsider. Whatever it is that you're planning, don't do it," he begged me quietly.

"What else am I supposed to do?!" I screamed, and my voice felt unrecognizable, shrill and suffocating. The turmoil inside me aided my mood swings. "I don't know what this is, or how to control it. I'm pretty sure it's controlling me at this point!"

"Wyatt," Lynx called, his voice assertive, but understanding. "You need to let this happen. If you refuse, you will condemn us all. You know that she will not be alone." His words reminded me that the three of us were in essence connected.

We should fight Alexandra together, but I was afraid of losing either of them.

"Emily, Wyatt, if we don't do this, we will lose ourselves to her. She will not take this lightly," Lynx warned as he looked at both of us.

"Emily... I can't lose you." His voice shook as an agony I'd never heard in it bubbled to the surface. He had been my rock, had kept me from losing my mind through so many years, and now it was my turn to do the same for him.

"You won't, Wyatt. We can do this. We can fight for our freedom together." My voice was quiet, but it rang with the power of our connection.

"Yes, Wyatt. You need to trust in all of us," Lynx chimed in, ever the mentor.

Wyatt

The lynx was right. I had to start trusting him, as well as give Emily the chance to do... whatever it was that she needed to. Even if I had to fight the urge to step in constantly. That would be difficult, because she was keeping her thoughts on this between the two of them. Not letting me in, when all I wanted to do was protect her. I felt like the odd man out. No, that wasn't right. I shouldn't fault Emily for not wanting to share everything with me. But what if what she was keeping between them was something dangerous? Something that could hurt her...

"Emily," I called to her, giving in to my uncertainties. "Please talk to me."

"I..." she began, quietly. "I have to stop her Wyatt, or else she will never stop coming after us."

"Agreed," I sighed. "But you can't do anything rash. And you can't... I mean you shouldn't do it on your own. You, Lynx, and I are a team, remember? We count on one another."

"But I don't want her to— I can't think of anything happening to you."

"She will hurt us regardless of how we react, but we'll be ready," I promised, reaching out to her. "We will fight her together. I can't promise you that nothing will happen to us," I added, reluctantly, "but we will all support each other."

"You're right," she sighed shakily, the ghost of a smile breaking through the fear in her voice.

"So, do you have any ideas on how to do this?" That seemed to be the question of the hour. Leave it to me to want to lead headfirst into something dangerous without a plan. "Impulsive as ever, I'm afraid," I joked. "Which wouldn't be ideal."

"Not at all," she giggled, lightening the atmosphere around us.

"Might I be of some assistance?" Lynx asked, joining in on our conversation.

Both Emily and I accepted, and he proceeded to explain his plan, which seemed confusing and difficult to follow at first, but once Emily and I started to pitch in ideas, the plan became our goal. It would be dangerous, but if nothing was risked, nothing would be gained. The least we could do was try to reach for our freedom.

Emily

I was making my way through pages, taking in the beauty that Wyatt and I had created for ourselves here. I may have added the visuals, but he seemed to breathe life into every one of my creations with his spirit and his faith. Maybe we could make a life for ourselves here. It wasn't like I had anything to go back to.

"You may have him now, but it won't be long before you turn, and there is nothing left of you. Everything that you have done will have been for nothing. I am already in your mind after all," Alexandra taunted.

But how?

"Oh, I think we both know the answer to that, Emily."

"You're trying to erase me," I concluded, and I could hear my heart pounding.

The dark presence I had come to know so well flowed like lava through me, burning me from the inside until there was nothing left. The fire produced a fog so thick that it coated everything around me like paint. It smelled like death. I knew it was only a matter of time before it overtook me. I couldn't help thinking about the others then. All the other girls that got trapped before me, who ended up lining Alexandra's bookshelves.

They'd scared me when I'd first heard them after Alexandra trapped me, their voices muted and sad. All of them had helped me though. They had kept me sane during my first years trapped in this place. They had even gotten me out of my head long enough for me to notice Wyatt. They had all faded with time, leaving me alone to watch over him, and I knew that one day I would fade away too. That I would become just another book. Dead pages without meaning.

"That will not happen. Don't let your mind get the best of you, Emily," Lynx encouraged, and I felt my walls crumble as they gave way to the tears they had been keeping back.

"It's just so much, Lynx. I'm surrounded by what I can become, and I'm terrified! You felt her, didn't you?" My thoughts weren't making sense. They felt angry and jumbled, and I couldn't focus on anything at all. Everything was just one giant mess.

"This will not happen to you, Emily. I can feel it. You are different. You have become the key that will set us all free," he soothed, bringing me back from the brink of panic.

"How?" I scoffed, the question almost breaking my voice. "What does that even mean?"

"The others did not have the support that you do. I was not there to help them, but I can rectify that now, by helping you and Wyatt," he replied almost shamefully.

"What if we lose you?" I asked, voicing one of my biggest fears. "What if something goes wrong and—"

"You must have faith, Emily. Trust in us and in our bond. I know that you can feel it. But above all, you must trust yourself."

"I do," I shivered, feeling the bond ebb and flow like gentle waves within me.

"I have also been doing a little work of my own," he said, with a mischievous but awkward tone to his voice.

"What?" I asked, suspicious.

He sent me images, memories of him mourning the deaths of Alexandra's previous victims, and vowing to avenge them as he absorbed their essences. The traces of the lives that she'd stolen.

"Wait, you mean to tell me that they didn't fade away?" I asked, and hope threatened to break my voice, but I reined it in.

"I'm afraid that some of them did," he regretted. "Too much time had passed and they—"

"No!" I cut him off, and the word left me feeling raw and exposed. My mind immediately started playing with me, bombarding me with thoughts of me ending up like the others. And no matter how many times he tried to convince me of the opposite, my mind wouldn't budge. My fear started to change though, anger taking its place when I thought about every life she had stolen, even if I couldn't find it in me to begrudge her my father's fate.

"You're torn," Lynx sensed, tilting his head. He looked so cute. "You hate her, but you're grateful to her as well."

The concern he had for me was obvious in his tone, and I was thankful again that I had found such a good friend. That he'd found me. "I am grateful to her in a way," I admitted. "I mean, if

137

all of this hadn't happened to me, I would have probably stayed with my father longer than I did, and would've paid the price. So I guess Alexandra saved me in a way. And then there's the fact that I never would've met you or Wyatt, and I can't see my life without either of you in it."

I felt him rub himself on me then, his purring reverberated through to my chest. The contact was comforting to both of us, and it seemed to energize me like a battery. Strength radiated through me. I felt like I could do anything in that moment.

"What is that?" I breathed.

"This is one of the ways that I can help you defeat Alexandra," he said and sent a powerful jolt through me that seemed to warm my entire being.

Not at all like the burning I felt from Alexandra's magic. This was soothing, and it energized me from the tips of my toes, to the top of my head. As it reached my heart, it turned into a gentle hum that resonated in my mind. "Is that you too?" I wondered out loud, listening to the lilting music.

"Yes, do you like it?" he answered, sounding self-conscious.

"Singing competitions would kill for something like this," I joked, earning a confused expression from him. "Never mind. It's beautiful, really."

There was an almost awkward pause between us then, and I had to confirm what felt inevitable.

"So... we really need to fight her, don't we?" I asked, but I was pretty sure I already knew the answer.

"It is the only way, Emily," he agreed. "But we will be together when that moment come. I promise you."

"Okay," I sighed. "We'll do it then."

The merge was happening. It had been slow at first, and therefore maddeningly undetectable, but as time wore on I could feel the surge getting stronger. There was some kickback, as was to be expected, but that would fade over time, because the wretch was not strong enough to wield my powers. She would succumb to them in the end. Just as I did.

I gasped when I woke up, because Alexandra's words were circling around in my mind, and I choked on the knowledge that my time was almost up. I knew that she was killing me slowly, snuffing me out undetected, and that she would likely replace me in such a way that Wyatt and Lynx would be none the wiser.

No, they would know that wouldn't be me, I reasoned with myself. *They have to.*

"Do you really think that they will be able to tell? I mean, we're so alike at this point, that I doubt they could tell the difference," she taunted, rocking my conviction.

"They have to," I defended, but my confidence was slipping, and she knew it.

"You're not so sure though, are you?" she prodded, her voice oozing with triumph as shame stole my voice.

The truth was that I wasn't. Not because of Wyatt or Lynx, but because Alexandra had done so much already to chip away at my faith. What would stop her from replacing me when she'd already taken over my life? What was to stop her from stealing the only two people I had left? The dark feelings that surfaced in me were evidence enough. I—We had to stop her for good, because I knew that she wouldn't be satisfied with my life. That she would get tired of it and go on to find another girl's life to steal.

"Yes, I am!" I yelled, fighting to break her hold on my consciousness and get back to my friends.

"Emily!" Lynx called out to me, breaking through the madness. "What happened to you?"

"Lynx!" I gasped, feeling tears of relief pooling up in my voice. "How did you find me?"

"I heard you fighting with her," he breathed, and started to purr to soothe my agitation. Its calming effect was almost instant, coaxing my breathing to follow his rhythm, slowing down after what felt like only a minute. His breathing also helped clear my mind of the fog that usually took over, letting me get my thoughts in order.

"Lynx, is there any way to break the connection?" I ventured, testing out my new theory.

He paused to think it over, and then gave me a short nod. "You must break all connections. Those with me and Wyatt as well."

That didn't sound good to me at all, and I could feel my heart getting ready to plummet. "What do you mean, break all connections? Like... I wouldn't be able to hear you anymore?"

"That is one of the scenarios, yes. And in losing your connection to Wyatt, he would lose his anchor..."

"No!" I interrupted. "I won't lose either of you!"

"Some sacrifices must be made to guarantee your freedom, Emily," he reasoned.

I didn't want to keep listening, because I refused to lose either of them. There had to be a way to keep them safe, and keep us together.

Wyatt

"I think you should listen to this, because it concerns you as well, Wyatt," the lynx's voice sounded in my mind as it tore the veil that kept my thoughts wrapped up.

"What...?" I called out, distracted. The rendering of the fabric allowed me to see what Emily had been trying to hide from me all this time. Everything was displayed in front of my eyes for the first time, and I hated myself for not noticing it all before. All of her pain, all of her disappearances, were caused by Alexandra. Would she always haunt us? We had to find a way to break her hold on us.

"There is a way," Lynx spoke suddenly, his tone grave. "There always has been, and you know it. Don't do anything stupid, Wyatt." He laughed and returned to Emily, giving me some much needed time to think.

I sighed reluctantly, and my mind rebelled against what was seeming more inevitable as time went on.

A sacrifice had to be made for our freedom, and I was afraid that the sacrifice would end up being one of us. The idea of dying didn't scare me, but thinking of either Emily or Lynx paying the price for all of this absolutely terrified me. Emily was my love, the one that had brought me back from the precipice that Alexandra was trying desperately to push me from.

And Lynx... Lynx had become like a brother to me, a wise voice that reined in my recklessness whenever it threatened either

Emily or myself. The conviction of knowing that I would sacrifice myself to save them without a second thought seemed to strengthen me and give me the bravery I needed to face our tormentor.

"Alexandra!" I called out to her, but got no response. She was clearly enjoying her game. Emily's presence was evident in that moment instead, and the calm that she provided helped to tone down my anger.

This calm turned to confusion however, when I turned around to see that there was no one there. "Emily? What are you doing?"

Giggles erupted in my mind, becoming louder as they continued. The tone was became darker, shifting from Emily's light and spirited laughter to something sinister that chilled me to the core.

"Hello, my love. It has been a long time since I've spoken to you."

I was so confused. It was Emily's voice in my head, that much was undeniable, but there was something that just wasn't right about it. The was only one possible option. "Alexandra," I answered as casually as possible, as I tried to disguise my emotions, which were starting to become haywire.

"Oh, you do remember me!" she cried out in a giddy, playful tone.

"How is this possible? Why are you doing this? Why can't you leave us alone?" I seethed, my emotions clearly getting the better of me.

"Oh, darling, I have been working on you for years. Did you really think that I would give up on you so easily?" she asked, trying to reason with me.

"Apparently not," I sneered. "But why hurt Emily? What has she done to deserve you doing this to her?"

"She has confused you and turned you against me. She stole the carrier from me. I need to get the both of you back," she explained, her voice ringing with jealousy. I couldn't take her smears against Emily any longer, but I would have to fight to keep my emotions in check.

"Carrier? Do you mean Lynx? So you're basically powerless...?"

"Not quite," she laughed, and a wave of pain came crashing over me. Its force stunned me, and I finally understood Emily, all the pain she had endured, and it only made me hate Alexandra more.

"You are deceitful," I growled, fighting the waves. I'd heard enough from her. "You kept me ignorant from the moment you created me. Had me follow after you like some mindless slave. And all for what? Love? You have no idea of what love really is." I hoped that my reproaches would work to distract her as I called for Emily and Lynx to join me in fighting her.

"Wyatt!" Both called out boisterously in my mind.

"Hang on!" Emily added.

Hang on? For what?

The answer to that came what felt like years later, when both of them appeared in front of me. My relief at seeing them was so great that I felt as if my breath had been knocked out of my chest.

"H-how?" I managed, dumbfounded.

"Neat, huh? The cat's really out of the bag now, I guess," Emily joked, but pride and excitement were obvious in her voice. "I decided to start practicing with these powers. No more being a coward. Want to see something else?"

I agreed carefully, and only when Emily had pointed did I become aware of Alexandra's frozen form in front of us, seemingly unaware of our exchange.

Emily then gestured between Alexandra and herself while looking at me as if I should be able to guess her meaning.

"Emily, you're going to need to be a little more specific, love," I huffed jokingly as I looked between her and Alexandra's frozen form. "Wait... How did that happen?" My tension eased somewhat at seeing Alexandra rendered immobile and seemingly non-threatening, but I remained on alert nonetheless as we left her presence.

"I did it!" Emily squealed, once we were safely away from Alexandra's frozen stare. "Well, Lynx and I did it actually. And if you help us, we can get rid of her for good!"

Hope and excitement surged within me, and threatened to overflow. Could we really get rid of our captor? "What do I do?" I asked.

"Are you ready to do whatever it takes?" Lynx asked, and I could feel his solemn stare on me as he joined us.

"Yes," I answered.

He nodded and pounced, leaving me breathless as he disappeared within me.

"What?" I gasped. "What is happening?!"

"He's merging with you. Helping Alexandra's magic within you come to the surface," Emily explained soothingly, and my strength began to come and go, leaving me drained.

I felt rooted in place as something began to shift within me. What could only be described as sharp tingles began to spread through me.

"That's what it feels like when your feet fall asleep," she commented casually, trying to keep me from panicking, even though her voice was riddled with tension.

I wanted to take that tension away, to help ease her, to vow to her that I would take all of her suffering from her from this moment on if need be, but I knew that she would have to conquer some things on her own at some point as well.

"Good man," Lynx approved as he pulled the veil between us and Emily to allow for privacy.

"You do know that's annoying, right?" I asked, and he laughed in response, giving me a playful nudge with his head.

"Relax, Emily knows how taxing this is. She knows that you need time to recuperate, and that we need time to work on our bond. She is very concerned about that."

He laughed indulgently, and again I felt as if I were being left out of a conversation that had everything to do with me.

"Not entirely," he conceded and I sighed, knowing that I would have to work for my privacy, but decided to be civil in this moment.

"Maybe she thinks we're at each other's throats right now," I laughed shortly.

"Quite possibly. Now rest," he whispered, and started lulling me to sleep.

I awoke what felt like hours later from a peaceful sleep, feeling Emily's presence by my side; her love for me was made obvious in the glow around her. "Good morning, sleepy head. Were you off at the boy's club?" She laughed.

"We were just talking about our issues, and working on the bonding thing," I explained, as I tried to get rid of my stupor.

Her smile broadened so much that it seemed to light the space around us.

"I guess you're happy about that."

"Very much so," she smiled. "I love you both."

"We love you too," Lynx said as he appeared, and enveloped us in an embrace.

Chapter 25

Alexandra

A glimpse. That was all I had managed since the wretch had blocked me out, and I had no doubt that the Carrier had helped her. That treacherous fur ball was toying with me, so I might just turn him into a wooden post for all his troubles.

Why go through all of this trouble if I could just create another lover? It was the principle of the matter.

I needed to recover that which was mine, even if I was to discard them and begin again. I would not allow anyone to have them either, because they were mine to do with as I pleased, and I wanted to end them for their disrespect.

They would all pay, once my transformation was complete. Once I took care of the usurper, nothing would stop me from living the life I had planned for myself. As the waves of power kept surging, I knew that it was only a matter of time.

"Alexandra," someone called my name, and I immediately knew who it was.

A smile tried to rise to the surface as the Carrier appeared in front of me, but I kept it at bay to play my role. "Have you come to beg for forgiveness? For mercy?" I asked, preening at the thought of his surrender.

"Yes, I have realized my mistake, and want to return to you," he replied quietly.

Emily

Lynx left us shortly after our talk, saying he had come up with a plan, and that he would let us know if anything happened. Wyatt and I stared at each other in confusion, and slight fear, but we trusted that he knew what he was doing. Still, the anxiety consumed me, because my worry for our friend grew more with each second he was away.

"Do you think...?" I began as I ran through possibilities in my head. "He's blocking me out and I can't sense him. Do you think she...?"

"I can't sense him either," Wyatt admitted, confused. "But wherever he is, I'm sure he's fine. He can take care of himself, Emily. I'm more concerned about us to be honest."

"I don't blame you, but I can't not worry about him, you know?" He then surrounded me in warmth, trying to soothe my ragged emotions. "He will be fine, Emily. I believe that, and so should you."

"I know, but you don't know how ruthless, how manipulative, she can be. I've seen that side of her for years!" My breath was coming faster and faster as my emotions escalated. That was when the buzzing began and radiated through me. This again?

"The powers are likely linking to your emotions," Wyatt reasoned through the chaos. "All the more reason to stay calm and analyze the situation."

"Yes, master," I mocked, amazed at what was happening, my strength increased by the second. Then I felt a familiar brush up against me. "Lynx!" I gasped, happy to feel his presence with me again, but something felt off. "Lynx, what's going on?"

"I'm afraid it can't answer you now," Alexandra answered instead, her voice drifting to me on the wind.

"What have you done to him?" Wyatt growled, apparently hearing her too. I was relieved that I wouldn't have to face her alone this time, but I was also worried about what had happened to Lynx.

"Oh, it's gone," she brushed off. "I got rid of it quite easily really, and it was so repentant too. It really was a shame."

I felt my world cave in around me when I heard those words. Lynx was dead. She had taken another important being away from me, and I had to make her pay. For Lynx. For Wyatt. For all the others she'd trapped. And especially, for me. My powers surged with the anger and pain I was feeling; traveling with a glowing warmth through me and into Wyatt, who wore the same determination on his face as I did. Our joined power just seemed to keep growing, almost becoming too much to handle, and I felt as if it were coming out of my pores.

Concentrate, Em, I told myself, and sent the same message to Wyatt, feeling his agreement as the energy held steady. He looked over at me, and his renewed concentration strengthened the bond even more.

His pained cry filled me with dread, and I reached out to him, recognizing his pain all too well. Alexandra was burning him from the inside out, just like she used to torture me.

When I felt him start to writhe from the pain, I fought the fear and desperation. "Lynx, what can I do?"

"You'll have to get her attention, Emily. Distract her."

I nodded, quickly. I would not run anymore. I would fight to protect the ones I loved, and avenge the ones I had lost. "Alexandra, stop! You want to fight? Then fight me! Leave Wyatt out of this."

"Oh, I will," she seethed, and her voice sounded distorted from rage, "but first he has to atone for his errors."

I didn't know how, but in that moment, I was able to sense her attacks before they happened. I reached out to Wyatt, hoping that my strength would be enough to help him resist what was coming.

"Be ready. Focu—" I didn't even get the words out before I felt him seize, his pain a near perfect copy of mine.

Alexandra was attacking us both, using our connection against us as punishment. I caught her off guard though, when I effectively shielded us both through the bond, pissing her off.

"Hey, Alex!" I called out to her, feeling a little smug. "You know what happens when you feel pain for so long? You build resistance to it."

I pushed all my emotions toward her in that moment, all of the pain and anger she had caused me throughout so many years, as Wyatt charged the attack. As she screamed, thick smoke began to take over everything, black and heavy enough to choke on. She was definitely pulling out all of her tricks, but they didn't affect me anymore.

"Wyatt, are you with me?" I asked.

"Always," he replied.

"As am I," I heard Lynx whisper, making me gasp and almost break into tears.

He was alive, safe, and... Wait... "H-how are you h-here? I thought s-she'd killed you," I rambled through breaths that made my chest feel tight, and my tears finally started to fall.

"Please... I was able to get away before she could. She isn't too happy though," he offered, and twitched his tail in her direction almost undetectably, freezing her on the spot.

"You don't say," Wyatt commented sarcastically, looking between him and Alexandra, earning a mild shove from me.

"Yes Wyatt, I do," Lynx reasoned. "In fact... she may or may not have followed me here. I don't know. Maybe I was too focused on getting away. Now, can we get back to the business at hand, please?" he asked, looking at Alexandra with a hatred that was very much palpable. It seemed so jarring and unexpected coming from him, because he was always so calm, but I knew that the hatred had been earned, and that it was completely justified. Even if I couldn't keep feeding that flame. "Give me some of your magic," he ordered, and Wyatt and I looked at each other with confusion, wondering what Lynx had up his sleeve. "Now!"

Both Wyatt and I extended our power, and as Lynx siphoned some of it into him, he seemed to grow bigger and more feral. He became so wild that he was almost unrecognizable as he looked from us to her.

He'd obviously sensed my panic, because he started whispering calming words to me through our bond. When he was satisfied that he had enough, I felt him break my connection to him. Then he ran away from me and into Alexandra, leaving me feeling empty and breathless.

"Lynx!" I managed to get out in spite of my shock and fear for him, but it was too late. He was already gone.

"Emily, focus!" Wyatt called out to me, reclaiming my attention.

"What do we do?!" I cried out desperately. "He's gone!"

"We can't worry about him right now!" he told me as he pointed to a twitching Alexandra. "And you know that he wouldn't want us to either. We have to get away from her!"

"No! I'm tired of running, Wyatt. She's taken too much from me, from us, and she's tormented me for long enough. I want her gone." My voice rang with a bravery I hardly recognized. I was looking for retribution for everything that Alexandra had done.

"What do I do?" Wyatt asked, sensing the change.

"You have to join me and Lynx. We have to combine our powers to be able to defeat her," I explained urgently, but had no idea where the answer came from.

I could tell that he thought I was going crazy just from the way he looked at me, and I didn't know if I could contradict him.

"Now!"

He reached out to me, trusting me wholeheartedly, and our bond seemed to intensify to a level I had never experienced. It felt like Alexandra's electricity, but it wasn't harmful at all. It was warm, familiar, and alive. I closed my eyes and felt his presence within me.

"Lynx?" I called out in my mind, and waited for a reply with bated breath. "Wyatt?" Neither of them answered, and after moments of silence that stretched out, I started to panic.

What happened to them? Where were they? That was when I glanced back to where Alexandra stood writhing. And I wished I could be the one causing it as payback for everything she had done to me. To all of us.

"No, Emily, please don't think like that. Don't think like her," Wyatt soothed, breaking through my thoughts, his voice a physical caress that made me shiver.

"You're okay!" I cried out in relief.

"Of course I am. You know that I'd never leave you," he laughed. "And neither would Lynx. He's here too." I breathed a sigh of relief that shifted to tears almost instantly.

"So, wait.... You're both in my head now?"

"It seems that way," he laughed, and it sounded like a reflex.

I was so focused on what that could possibly mean, that I completely missed Alexandra's unfreezing, and the fact that she was creeping up to us, shifting the air around us and turning it to a chaotic storm. Oh, great.

"I do believe that belongs to me," she commented, and her voice was a full blown threat now. She obviously didn't care about pretending anymore.

"H-how did y-you...." My words stumbled. "I thought that Lynx froze you!"

"Stupid girl. This just shows how unfocused and ill equipped you are to wield my magic," she gloated. "You clearly don't deserve it. Why don't you disappear as you should have long ago, and let me handle it?"

"Enough!" Wyatt yelled, his voice breaking through Alexandra's influences like a sword slashing through a veil.

"And that is why I could never give up on you," she remarked, and her voice overflowed with pride and obsession. "You have a mind of your own, and you don't conform to what you are told. You're perfect."

"You just realized this, huh?" I remarked sarcastically, hoping that Wyatt caught on to my diversion, and used this time to attack.

"Allow me, I've had enough of her to last me twenty lifetimes," Lynx said smugly, and attacked her with the combination of all of our powers.

The strength of the onslaught was almost enough for me to feel pity for her. Key word, almost.

"Kill her, Lynx," I growled, releasing all the anger and sadness I'd accumulated throughout the years. "But be careful."

As I looked on, I could see straight through Alexandra, could feel her drowning in the magic she'd once reveled in as it rolled onto her like ocean water, could feel her fighting against it. But like rogue ocean waves, it wasn't long before they overpowered her. When those receded, I saw her lifeless body, my lifeless body, laying in front of me. I couldn't help crying when I saw it, from relief, from anger, and from insecurity.

"We are not done yet!" Lynx called out to us, seemingly ready to attack again, but he didn't use our magic, and instead he shook himself as if he was waking up from a deep sleep.

I looked on confused, until I saw the spirits of all of Alexandra's victims rising from him like smoke. They seemed understandably livid and hungry for revenge as they seeped into her, each one dealing out their own punishment to her.

Alexandra seemed to be fading right in front of me, like I was watching a slide show of all the stages of decay; I won't lie and say that it didn't make me nauseous.

"Go, now!" they all cried out at once, snapping me back to my reality. I nodded and left as fast as I could, dragging Lynx and Wyatt away with me.

"What's going to happen to them? Are they going to be alright?" Wyatt asked, once we had gotten away.

"They chose to sacrifice themselves for us, because they knew that they had no chance of living outside of these books, and they wanted to give you both the opportunity to live. Don't question their gift. Accept it," Lynx said sagely.

"He's right," I cut in, tears hollowing out my voice. "Don't let their bravery be in vain."

"What happens now?" Wyatt asked after a while, his words echoing my thoughts.

"I have no idea," I replied, feeling like I was coming out of a fog. My thoughts spun.

"I thought the next step would be obvious..." Lynx remarked happily. "Emily, you can recover your body now."

His words knocked the air out of me. This had been the one thing I'd wanted for so long, and now that I was getting it, I was stalling. "But wait, what about you and Wyatt?"

"We'll have to stay here," Wyatt answered, deceptively nonchalant. "There's no way for us to leave this place, Emily, but you can get back to your life."

"Wyatt, you forget that you and Lynx are my family. Apart from you two, I have no one," I reminded him, the pang of loneliness hitting me hard.

"I never said anything about leaving you, Emily," Lynx soothed. "Remember that you carry us with you."

Wyatt

Her demeanor changed immediately, the power seemed to shift with it as it came out of her, searching for something. When she spotted her body lying on the floor, a sense of determination took over.

"Go, Emily," I encouraged.

"Come with me," she said, her nervous excitement palpable.

"I will follow you anywhere," Lynx vowed, and I smiled in agreement.

Together, the three of us walked off the page, and into her body.

THE END

About the Author

    Gabriela Bianchi is 30% human, 30% cyborg, 30% writer of YA, and 10% funny. She lives in Puerto Rico, and has spent most of her life enamored by books, because they were a way for her to distract herself from her condition of Hydrocephalus. So much so that she decided to become a writer herself.

Gabriela Bianchi

From Three Furies Press:
https://threefuriespress.com/

Spade
S.L. Byrum

Pain.

How easily we address it in others, yet so often we deflect it
in ourselves. At least. That's the case with the Plachette family,
having just suffered a loss of a beloved wife and mother, Kathy.

Henry and his daughter must shoulder their grief and carry
on, though chaos threatens to overtake them at any moment. As
luck and legacy would have it, they are not alone in their struggle; a healing realm awaits them both on the tattered edges of the
dream world and reality.

Spade, the conduit between the healing realm and human reality, has returned to warn, instruct, and to fight for them both,
though her preference for the forest animals is hardly a secret.
Henry and Drea must face their inner chaos in the dream realm
to heal or succumb to an alluring fate of eternal emptiness. They
are not alone in their battle, but the parallel between fantasy and
reality will be questioned every step of the way.

Out of the London Mist
Lyssa Medana

When news of his brother's murder reached him, aether pilot John Farnley raced back to his old family home.

While he comforts his bereaved sister-in-law, and tries to sort the family business and holdings, he also wonders why his brother, Lord Nicholas Farnley, had ventured into the cramped streets of the East End of London where he had met his violent end. The slums are a deadly place where life was cheap and murderous thugs preyed on the weak and lost.

Now, in the midst of a thick, London fog, something even more monstrous is waiting in the mist-shrouded shadows. Something that has been brought to life by the refugees crowding Bethnal Green and Mile End. Something his brother might have had a hand in creating.

Aided by his friend, the resourceful Miss Sylvia Armley, his own understanding of the aether lines that flow above London, and guided by the erudite advice of Professor Entwistle, John is forced to find his way through the darkest part of London to avenge his brother and stop whatever aether powered monster is lurking there.

Moss and Clay
Rebekah Jonesy

Moss, Clay, and Blood

A doll, crafted and given a mission by Danu, is brought to life by human and fae blood. Blood daughter of Mab, Queen of the Fae, Gillian must track down the fae in the Americas and bring them back under Fae Law. No one knows what is holding them there, or why no other rescue mission has returned. Not even the gods that sent them. Gillian must return the fae to the Underhill, or send them back to Danu.

Ren the Red Falcon
Joshua Robertson

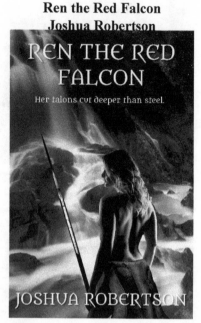

Taken by Aggath slavers as a child, Ren's youthful rage was tempered by the crack of a whip.

Season after season, she endured the wrath of those who slaughtered her kin and stole her life. Years later, when her captors are unexpectedly defeated by a company of savage barbarians, Ren briefly tastes freedom before being ensnared once more to be gifted to another tribe as a token of peace. Now, with thralldom threatening her future once more, she must learn to rekindle her inner fire or forever suffer a life of servitude.

Read Me

The Suffering
Robert Cano

After twelve long years of ongoing warfare between the Fae and the Satyrs in her kingdom, Devani is finally heading home. The war was on the doorstep of her father's land when she was sent to stay in Yor'lon, where the king and queen were supposed to treat her kindly. The war has shifted now, and it is time to go home.

But the princess soon finds herself in a position she never expected, especially so close to returning. Struggling against death itself, her will to survive is overwhelming. She finds a way to freedom and relative safety, but at what cost and for how long? It seems the gods have other plans for Devani.

Augur of Shadows
Jacob Rundle

Destiny. Adventure, Prophecy.

Grief-stricken, seventeen-year-old Henri moves to New York City after he loses his father. Vivid dreams and visions lead him to meet a wise young man, Simeon, someone who means more to him than he wants to admit. He also reconnects with an old friend, Etlina.

The three of them venture on a journey to fulfill their inter-twined destinies in order to bring forth a cataclysmic event that's meant to hold back the Primordial Evil.

With guidance from supernatural beings, Henri and his friends will do what is needed to save the world from the Old Ones.

Road to Jericho
Mark Reefe

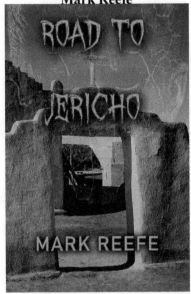

No good deed goes unpunished.

Finn McCallan is a genuinely good man. The type of man who steps in and helps when he sees a dying woman. But his good deed draws the ire, and interest, of the devil whose plan he thwarted. Wearing the mask of a human named Leonard, the devil tricks Finn into a deal, which leaves him marked.

The brand in the center of his right palm isn't the worst of it. His eyes can see the true face of everyone he encounters - frightening him more than anything in life had prior.

Now no matter how far he runs, how determined he is to lay low, calamity seeks him out.

Torturing him, testing him, provoking him. Destroying everything good in his life. He will not be allowed to live a peaceful life until the bargain is fulfilled. To what end?

And for what purpose?

Only the devil knows, and he's not telling.

Gabriela Bianchi

Read Me

Gabriela Bianchi

Read Me

Gabriela Bianchi

CPSIA information can be obtained
at www.ICGtesting.com
Printed in the USA
BVHW081326310821
615689BV00002B/121

9 781950 722853